WICKED PRINCE

BOOK TWO IN THE TERRITORIAL MATES SERIES

MARY E. TWOMEY

For Ilyssa Morgan,

Who carves her own destiny,
and lights the paths of everyone she meets.

BLUE EYES, TEDDY BEAR

DESTINO

My wife drools in her sleep. I don't know why I find this hilarious, but I can't stifle my snigger when I round the corner and see her with her arm extended across the table in the back corner of the library of the castle. Her lavender curls are sprawled out on the desktop, her plump lips open just enough for me to catch the glimmer of drool trailing down the corner of her mouth.

"Did she fall asleep?" King Ronin asks as he comes to stand beside me, juggling three leather-bound books.

Great-grandfather, not King Ronin. Because apparently, we're all familial now, so maybe I don't need to use his title. Maybe I'll go with calling him just plain Ronin, like Lily's been bold enough to do.

My smile fades and my back straightens as I nod. It's my hope I can convince us both that I'm a man fit for ruling someday, and not his goofball great-grandson who's only good for making the nation laugh and swoon.

I try not to let it matter that my great-grandfather is watching my wife sleep. There's something too intimate about the way he watches her. I know that look. It's almost the same one I wear when my eyes wander to Lily, as they often do. Great-grandfather and I could pass for brothers, maybe even twins, though he won't leave his room unless the sharp edge of his jaw is cleanshaven, and I keep tight to my neatly groomed five o'clock shadow. Though King Ronin's been frozen to look in his young thirties like me, he's decades older than that, and should know better than to gaze at Lily like that. She's *my* wife, not his.

And soon she'll be Alex's wife, too. Sharing her affections with my best friend doesn't bother me one bit. Anyone else, though, and I become a possessive wanker. It's not a gracious color on me.

Carefully as I can, I lift the hand that's resting atop the book she's fallen asleep on and curl her slender arm around my neck. Though I'm fluid with my movements, she startles when my arms tuck under her thighs and behind her back, lifting her from the hard-backed wooden chair. Her eyes open as she swipes at the corner of her mouth. "Oh! Did I… I did it again, didn't I."

"Fell asleep studying? It's the second time this week, but a vampire's schedule isn't easy to adopt. Up all night and sleeping during the day is a hard transition."

"I'm awake now. I can study some more."

She finds my smile, even when she's not trying to. "The

sun's shining, so upstairs we go. Any morning I get to carry you to bed is a good one in my book."

"Mm. It's quiet," she comments as we make our way out of the library, leaving King Ronin and the entirety of my family's collections of books behind us for a few hours.

"The protesters have gone home. Probably because they finally adore you as much as I do now."

She doesn't buy my white lie. "Ha, ha. They've only stopped shouting curses at me because the sun's up and they have to go indoors. They're refueling for tonight when they can start fresh. I do hope they find a better rhyme for my name, though. Silly? Filly? It's like they're not even trying. I think it's because they secretly love me."

I love that she's thick-skinned enough to make a joke of their hatred. If there's anything that seals her as the one for me, it's the fact that she can find cause to make light of even the most dire of circumstances.

None of us assumed the news of our secret wedding would go over without a hitch. The vampire prince marrying a fae cast-out from Neutral Territory is unheard of. Still, I'd hoped the people would love me more than they hate her, and eventually they could grow to be tolerant of us. Perhaps a month's time is too much to expect for total acceptance.

Climbing stairs while carrying a woman is no small feat, but she's just sleepy enough not to struggle out of my arms. I make sure not to grunt when I get halfway up the winding staircase. She smells like peaches and actual lilies, and though I've never been big into picking flowers, I can't believe my good fortune that this one gets to be mine.

Laying her down in my bed—*our* bed—is something that makes my chest expand. I'm not sure what the tipping point was that switched us from a marriage made to piss off the masses to actual affection. Maybe it was how gently she held me in the weeks following my father's death, or how she stood by my side with Salem and Alex through the funeral, enduring the hatred of hundreds of thousands of vampires with a raised chin that scolded them all not to bother us with such things when I was clearly grieving. She never told me how to feel, or made me talk about the things that were too big to put words to.

Lily makes me cookies. She calls them her ugly cookies, and the blobby lumps live up to the name. But they take away the nightmares I can't otherwise escape. Over and over, I see Ronin stabbing my father with a silver blade, and then cuffing the back of his neck and hurling him over the balcony. Though father and I were never close, it's a hard image to escape. I had my doubts that a simple cookie could lessen my pain, but Lily promised they would keep the nightmares away, and she was right.

The ugly cookies are just the tip of her kindness. Lily looks after me when I'm not sure which way is up anymore. She calls my people "our people," which is just about the most gracious thing she can say about a group that loathe the sight of her.

So I keep the death threats away from her ears as much as I'm able, shielding her just as she's stood in front of me when life proves it doesn't know how to be gentle with the fragile parts of us.

My own mum still hasn't spoken to me—too angry that I've besmirched our family's good name by marrying outside my race. I'm sure not many newlywed men are grateful to spend their time alone with their wife blubbering into her breasts, but laying in bed with Lily, I know that's where my head belongs, and she's never begrudged me the pleasure.

I take off her shoes and socks, loving that she lets me do these simple things for her. I've been studying with King Ronin in a separate part of the library for hours, taking careful notes while he pours his decades of ruling knowledge into me. Lily's still catching up on vampire history, insisting she needs to know how we got to this boiling point if she's to understand how we'll move forward towards a brighter future.

Now that I'm near her and away from the duty of it all, I ache to be closer. My house has never felt so cold as it does when I know there's finally a source of warmth inside, but it's just out of reach.

Her eyes are lidded when she gets off the bed, selects a pair of pajamas and slips into the bathroom to change. I take my time getting undressed, stretching out my neck, which is sore from so much reading. I never thought King Ronin would consider giving up the throne, and I really never assumed he would pick me. I always thought he hated me. I'm the laidback one, when he's always so very cunning and calculating. Ever since he made the announcement that I will be next to rule after a year of instruction, he's been adamant I learn every detail of how he wants things to be run after he steps down. I'm glad for the training, of course, but thirteen hours of constant study is a good recipe for a crick in my neck.

Lily meanders out in a pink thermal t-shirt and gray flannel pants. The fae are known for their trickery, but there's no guile in the simple clothing. In fact, her drawer is stocked with far racier sleepwear (I made sure of it). Being fae, she chills easily in our colder climate. She chooses practicality over appearance, and yet somehow still emerges with such appeal that I have to remind myself to behave.

"Sorry, let me put on my pants." I'm in my boxer briefs, but she gives a nonplussed shrug.

"Sleep however you're comfortable. We're in this for the long haul, remember."

"Perfect woman, you are."

"Remember you said that when I can't recall whole chunks of your Drexdenbergian history, and make myself look like an idiot in front of the territory." She flops sideways onto the bed, spreading her arms out like a starfish as she stares at the ceiling. "I haven't had to study anything since I was a little girl. I'm sorely out of practice."

"When do you imagine you'll be quizzed publicly on something like that?"

A yawn slips from her mouth, tilting her chin. She's like a kitten, figuring out how best to fall asleep on the thick bedding.

"Your feet are icy," I comment, rubbing her toes to heat them. I'm acutely aware of how next-to-naked I am, and that this is perfectly fine with us both.

She flips down the comforter. "Then come be my furnace."

A wicked smile curves my lips. "If you insist." She doesn't pull away when I climb in and lay next to her, my hands slipping under her shirt so they can slide up and down along her spine. Drexdenberg is cooler than what most fae can handle, though she never complains. We usually sleep with our heads on the pillows and her left hand on my chest, and I love it.

I've never been one for keeping a woman in my bed for just plain sleep, but I've grown rapidly addicted to having my sheets smell like lilies. Sometimes we kiss once before we close our eyes, but today Lily has other plans. She snuggles into my arms, her stomach tight to my abdomen as her lips find mine in the windowless dark.

I was so afraid she'd recoil at my fangs, but now her tongue teases the tips. I'd never bite her, never hurt her, and she trusts me enough to know that. Fae don't normally touch vampires, yet this kitten practically purrs when she loops her leg over mine, bringing my thigh between hers. She's usually tentative in her seduction, dipping her toe in before delving into a full-on makeout. Guess I'm just lucky today, so I don't question it. Instead I roll her onto her back, kissing her so hard, her toes curl on the backs of my calves.

I'm her first boyfriend. I have to remind myself of that

fact over and over when I want to tear her clothes off and see just how far she'll let me take this whole marriage thing. A few months ago, she'd never kissed a man, yet here we are, twisting in the sheets like teenagers. We've built something solid we can lean on when the world throws its stones, and in the dark, we remind each other of our bond that's strong, but still so very new.

"I love you in my bed," I breathe between kisses.

"I love you in my arms," she replies, running her nails up my sides. She bunches them in my hair and gives a little tug, which she knows by now is a trigger for me. My whole body hums for her little touches and teases. So much of our life is hard, but this feels easy, and I love it. Though she's new at kissing, she takes to the art like a pro, letting me guide her when she's nervous.

When she pulls back, her eyes meet mine with something she doesn't let anyone else see. There it is, my little gift all wrapped up in the most unlikely package. Vulnerability. That's what she gives only me. Even with Alex, she tries to play the role of a confident fae woman. With Salem, she can barely look at him without getting too anxious to speak. But she hands me her vulnerability because she knows I'll be gentle with it. I'll be gentle with her.

So I slow our kiss without sacrificing any of the heat we both crave. My body sinks atop hers as I suck on her lower lip. I reach down and grip under her knee, pulling her leg to curve next to my hip. Though she's fully clothed, her breath hitches when my palm slides with painstaking purpose up her thigh, thumbing the inner curve the entire way. I want her little mewls of pleasure, so I kiss her lips each time one escapes, trapping it in my teeth so I can keep it. Because it's mine. *She's* mine. And somewhere along the way, I became hers.

It's me who has to stop twenty minutes later, or I know I'll take things farther than she's comfortable. I roll off of her and talk myself down while I stare up at the dark wood slats of the ceiling. "You're trouble, blue eyes. I was all set to go to bed a gentleman, but you seduced my shirt and pants right off of me."

She struggles to catch her breath through her giggle. "You know us tricky fae. Always up to something." She straightens her shirt that I managed to twist up around her ribs. "Any word from Lexi?"

You would think mention of my best friend right after a makeout that intense would be a mood killer, but I find it doesn't bother me. Her hand crawls its way to my chest and she exhales, like her ring knows it belongs over my heart. Her pale flesh nearly glows in the dark, starkly contrasting my vampiric olive skin. "No word yet. But that's not abnormal. It's almost a week's journey by carriage from my castle to his. Plus, it's a lot of covert trickery he's got to do, figuring out if we're being shorted on blood shipments from the fae, who's responsible, and how to handle it. Plus, I'm sure news of his engagement is causing all sorts of stir."

She exhales, her breath teasing the tuft of dark hair on my chest. There it is again, that vulnerability. I tuck my arm under her neck so she can rest her head on my shoulder, and I can hold her as close as possible. My touch unlocks her worries, which tumble out of her in a rush. "I'm not ready to leave. I like it here with you."

It's not what I expect her to say, especially with the mob greeting us outside the castle grounds when we wake every night. "I like you here with me, too. Do you not want to marry Alex?"

She keeps her mouth shut tight for a few seconds, and I can tell she's weighing her words. "I do. There's just a lot more to all of this than I realized. Plus, your people are incredible. Did you know that Edmund Waters saved a hundred and three people who were on the brink of starvation by slitting his own wrists in tiny cuts to feed his town? He bled himself dry for his people. That was during the siege of the Sanders Prairie. I can't believe the shifters blocked off your borders like that for months, and the fae refused to send their regular shipments of filtered blood."

My brows furrow. "Doing a bit of light reading, I see?"

"I don't know how you all survived it. So horrible!"

"Yes, well the shifters have a very different account of how all that went down. Apparently, we started it."

Her dainty nose scrunches. I like when it does that. "Huh? Your history book clearly says it was an unprovoked attack."

"You'll have to ask Salem all about it. Or you can ask his brother."

"What's his brother's name again?"

I chuckle. "Justice."

"But I'd like to actually know his full name. Give me the whole thing. Prince Justice Twinkletoes Butcher? Prince Justice Super-Nice-Guy Butcher?"

"It's something like fourteen names long. I'm too tired to get them all right now."

"And Prince Salem, what are all of his names?" Her voice is always timid when she talks about him. It's cute.

"Prince Salem Butcher. That's it."

Again with the nose crinkle. It's bloody adorable. "That hardly seems fair. Why should Prince Justice get all the fancy names but Prince Salem only gets the one?"

"Imagine being in primary school, having to spell out all of those names. Salem got a lucky break, if you ask me. His father loved Justice more, and his mum loved them both equally. You'd think the two would've been enemies, but they get along brilliantly. Salem never cared about titles or prestige. He just wants the job done, to do right by his country."

"He's noble. How about Prince Justice? Is he a good man?"

I shrug. It doesn't bother me to talk about Alex or Salem in bed with her, but Justice? I don't want his mug swimming around in my head before I drift off. "Of course. You'll be safe in Jacoba."

Her hand slips from my chest. "I can tell that's not true." It's not a hostile accusation, but an observation as she shakes out her hand. "The ring practically bounced off your chest just now. It can tell when you're lying."

I frown down at the white gold band and lavender

stone. "Pesky bugger. I should've bought you a regular ring with no hints of magic. Then I could lie and tell you no one will ever come up against you. There are no wars. There is nothing that can hurt us."

"It's okay. You don't have to tell me more."

"How about I tell you that it's time to sleep, and conversations like these are only going to keep you awake."

Her hand migrates back to my chest, where it belongs. I grip her wrist so I can kiss her fingertips. Each kiss melts away a little of her unease as her body relaxes once more against mine. "You're probably right."

"I usually am. Annoying habit of mine. Goodnight, blue eyes."

She pecks my cheek and says quietly, "Goodnight, teddy bear."

I hate the nickname, but I am completely and wholly in love with her.

I can only hope that one day, my people won't spend their time shouting for my wife's swift death.

2

WALTZ AND WARNING

LILYA

I hold up my hand to stave off Des' forthcoming protest. "I've got fancy dresses packed in my suitcase. I'm not traveling in those. If someone aims an arrow at you, I don't want to trip when I knock them out. Undermines the whole don't-mess-with-my-man thing if I fall on my face."

Des sniggers, as if I'm trying to be funny or something. Jeans and a long-sleeved t-shirt are the way to travel, plus my dagger with silver spikes ready to foist out from the hilt strapped to my thigh holster. "Alright, but the people are used to Mum when they see royalty. This might take them some getting used to." He motions to his mother, who's nursing her third cocktail in the past hour. Melinda looks meticulously put together in her red mid-calf dress, though on the edge of drunk, as she always looks.

She scoffs in my direction, leaning against the far wall

of the receiving room. "They would sooner accept a cow on the throne than that pale abomination."

I will myself not to think of all the ways I could retaliate. No one in Drexdenberg knows my magic is defunct; instead of the fruit trees and flowers every other fae can bloom, the only bits of nature I can conjure are poisonous plants. So I pretend I have no magical aptitude at all, that I'm stupid, and tuck away my urge to bloom a plant that could cause boils to sprout all over Melinda's foul tongue.

That would be bad.

It sets Des' teeth on edge whenever his mother takes a crack at me. I don't care if she ever likes me, but I hate what it does to Des. I step closer to him, pleading with my eyes for him to let it go. Yesterday featured an hour-long fight over dinner between the two of them when she'd called me her son's whore.

I force a smile and pretend we're only talking about the public, and not his own mother. "They'll never get used to me. Best be myself."

"Wise words, indeed," Ronin says, strolling through the opened door of the posh room I've only seen used for cocktails and subtle needling. He's wearing pressed black pants, a pinstriped vest over a white dress shirt and a black suit coat with a flash of emerald silk lining I catch sight of as he adjusts his cufflinks. "She'll be wearing a cloak anyway, Son." Then to me he adds, "Destino is particular about your attire because he doesn't want the people to assume you deserve less than any princess of Drexdenberg."

I try to keep my attitude in check, but it's like every day with these people, trying to dress me up, as if that's the thing that'll change people's minds. "Look, if the carriage gets highjacked, I highly doubt the sight of me in a dress will be the thing that gives them pause."

I don't want to go. I'm stalling, and everyone knows it, but I don't want to get in that carriage. It'll take me to Faveda, where I don't want to be. I wish I could keep Lexi without having to see my old homeland.

Or my father, who thinks I'm dead because he tried to make it so and didn't stick around to make sure the shifter that attacked me finished the job.

Melinda saunters past me and pretends to trip, dumping her blood martini down the front of my shirt. "Oops! How clumsy of me."

It's the third time she's done something like this, and each time, I try not to hate her for it. My hate doesn't do anyone a lick of good. I hated my father, and he still sits pretty in his position of political prestige. When I hate, it consumes only me, not the person who deserves it.

I swallow my shriek and hold the hem of my shirt out so I don't get blood stains on my jeans. "Good thinking, Mommy." Yeah, she gets real steamed whenever I call her that. "This color clashes with the bags of money I'm stealing from your family. I'll go change."

It's all I can do to keep my fingers from trembling as I scamper up the steps, leaving behind the sounds of Des and his mother fighting over how she treats me. I feel terrible for Des, championing this losing battle of trying to get her to respect me in any way. The second I cross over into my bedroom and shut the door, I whip my shirt over my head, trying to keep the blood away from my hair. The few guards I passed on my way up here didn't even raise an eyebrow at my blood-soaked form. It could've been a legit attack, and the crimson could've been from my own body, but they aren't worried. I'm sure if I ended up dead, that would make their lives far easier. Benny, Ronin's head of security, is the only one of them who treats me as if I'm a person worth guarding.

I take my time dabbing off the wetness from my chest with a washcloth that I've sufficiently ruined. I change my bra because that's a thing I can do now. Des ordered me one in every color, and some are too pretty to touch just yet. I put on a peach one that clashes a little with my hair, but makes me feel spectacular and busty.

I'm not prepared for a visitor, much less one who doesn't knock. When Ronin bursts through the bedroom door, I squeak and cross my arms over my chest.

Ronin stumbles backward, his eyes shooting skyward as he flings the door shut with him on the wrong side of it. "Oh! I'm sorry, Lilya."

"Get out!"

"Yes, I… Hold on. I'll fix this." He whirls around and opens the door, but slams it shut again. "Benny's in the hallway. Here." He slides off his suit jacket and vest, then unbuttons his shirt and flings it over his shoulder at me.

"Des bought me some clothes, but thanks."

"Yes, but if Melinda sees you in my shirt, she's less apt to 'accidentally' spill something on you again."

"Fair point." I scoop it off the ground and shove my arms into it, buttoning it as quick as my quaking fingers will allow. "Okay, I'm decent."

He clears his throat three times before slowly turning, his hands in his pockets and his eyes still on the ceiling. "I do apologize. I assumed you'd be washing off in the bathroom still. I was worried you were upset, so I came up here to…" He shakes his head. "If you could not mention this particular blunder, that would be most helpful."

I can't help my snigger at the pink in his cheeks. "Are you blushing? Well, that's just about the cutest thing. You look like a boy." Even his undershirt is pressed and perfect. Sheesh. I've never seen him like this, though. I could swear his pajamas are a fancy suit. His expensive pants and undershirt humanize him a little, making him look more like Des.

"Yes, well, I'm the king, and should know better than to burst into people's bedrooms unannounced."

"I'm dressed, you know. You can look at me."

It's an effort, and the ruddiness in his cheeks only blooms more furiously when his eyes finally descend to land on me. I cross my eyes to break the tension, which serves to loosen his shoulders with an airy laugh. "Are you alright, then? I came up to make sure you were okay, but managed to give myself a heart attack."

"I'll take that as a compliment. And I'm fine. Nothing

I'm not used to. Melinda does something like this just about every day."

"Melinda was out of line. When you return to me, I'll make sure she's better behaved. I've been looking the other way because, well, I killed her husband, but it stops now."

I fiddle with the too-long sleeves. "She'll always hate me because I'm fae. It's fine. People used to spill their ales on me all the time in the bar. Hilarious."

His mouth draws to the side. "That seems like a waste of perfectly good ale."

"You forget I was the only fae in Neutral Territory. Not exactly winning any popularity contests. Melinda's going to have to seriously up her game if she wants to take the prize for most humiliation she can dump out on me. I think I'm shock-proof by now."

My smile is flawlessly faked, but Ronin sees right through me. "Is that so?" He clears the gap between us and tugs at my sleeve, straightening it before rolling the cuff a few times so the shirt isn't as cumbersome. "If I didn't know better, I would think you're terrified to go home."

"I'm not going home. Neutral Territory is my home. Here is my home. I'm going to Faveda to visit, is all. It'll be fine."

He's quiet while he does the same to my other sleeve, taking his time and standing close enough that my lies are too loud to slip by unnoticed. "Destino won't tell me why you were kicked out of Faveda. Won't tell me a thing about your upbringing. Not who your parents are, not what crimes you committed to be sent there. Nothing. Either he's being a very good husband, or he doesn't know." His lower lip twitches, and I'm close enough to inhale the fancy cologne scent I love. There are notes of bergamot and fresh citrus in Ronin's aftershave. "I'm not in the habit of not knowing things, yet it appears that I'm constantly wondering, now that you're here."

I try to smile again, but it's a bad job. "Well, get used to being all-knowing again, because I'll be out of your hair in just a few minutes."

His mouth firms in a taut line as he folds the sleeve again. "Your education is lacking. Your handwriting is like that of a child. Who failed to raise you properly?"

It's not meant to be a dig, but it stings just the same. I was abandoned when I was eight years old. There aren't exactly primary schools in Neutral Territory. Fiora cared more about what asset my poison-by-plant ability proved than writing lessons and arithmetic and things like that. Numbers only mattered when I was adding up someone's tab, or measuring out ingredients for a charm. And who cares what a person's handwriting looks like?

Instead of letting my underbelly show, I roll my shoulders back and lift my chin. "We don't need to have this conversation." I try to jump away from that topic, keeping my tone breezy. "I made extra ugly cookies to hold you over while I'm gone. I know it's not Des eating them all. Do you want to talk about your nightmares?"

Ronin's frown tightens. "Not even a little bit. And I'll not let you change the subject. I was curious about your background before, but now you've got me concerned.

How did you get kicked out of Faveda? I checked with the fae prison logs, but there is no Lilya Klein who was charged with a crime who might be your age now. You can't have been kicked out of Faveda more than a couple years ago. You're still so young. And they've never sent anyone to Neutral Territory that I know of."

I listen to him work through his puzzle with no urge to solve it for him. "Sounds like you want to know things that're none of your business," I comment without bite in my tone. I am none of his business, except how I conduct myself in his kingdom. I haven't used my poison to kill anyone in Drexdenberg.

I haven't killed anyone that way in a while.

He walks in a slow circle around me, sizing me up and making me nervous. "What do you know of Faveda as it is today? You've been gone from there for so long."

I shrug. "Fae are supposed to be perfect. Clean and always wearing spotless white clothes to show off how unaffected they are by work or anything hard. They smile and then snipe. Appearances are important; people are not."

"Yes, it seems nothing's changed since you were there last. Do you know of the affliction they've come under in the past two years?"

I shake my head. "There aren't any Fae in Neutral Territory, aside from me. Not much news travels from there."

"It seems they've created something of a problem for themselves. It was supposed to be a monster born of their magic that could fight on their behalf, so they wouldn't have to get their hands dirty. They call it Gorgonell—an enormous bull with impenetrable, scaly skin. I'm told it's half the size of a house, and no one can get close enough to kill it."

I grimace. "What does it do, gore people to death?"

Ronin's eyes bore into mine as he comes full-circle to stand before me. "It turns to stone anyone who looks into its eyes."

A gasp flies from my lips. "That's awful! How did they even go about making something so horrible?"

"I would say to ask the creature's creators, but they've been turned to stone. The fae have always been curious about pushing the limits of magic. The vampires call it poetic that the Gorgonell never made it out of their territory, but turned on its makers. I'm inclined to agree."

Compassion floods me, and I feel terrible for saying disparaging things about them. "How many have been affected?"

"Dozens? Hundreds? I'm not sure. The Gorgonell comes out at dusk and doesn't wander far from his cave. There haven't been any incidents in months, but the fear is always there. Since the creature fears the light, I suspect they used vampire blood in its construction. You can imagine how I feel about that."

"I'm guessing you're not thrilled."

"Indeed. When you go to Faveda, I want you to stay away from the Stone Graveyard. That's the home they've given it to keep it far from the living. Promise me."

I nod. "Alright. I'm not exactly jonesing to go hang out

with someone who can turn me to stone with a single glance. That would put a serious damper on our plans to unite the territories."

"That, it would. I want nothing but fun for you, wherever you travel, so stay away from anything that might take you away from me."

Ronin's words are so to the point and grand that my breath stills in my chest. "I don't know what to say to that. Thank you."

"A thank you suffices." He smirks at the sight of me in his shirt and my jeans. "They'll throw a grand ball for Prince Alexavier and his fiancée. Do you know how to dance?"

Ronin takes my hand in his and holds it out to the side, his other touching down on the back of my hip. He starts out in a slow waltz, which I cannot believe I remember. It was so long ago that Lexi and I took lessons for his appearances at the grand balls. I still remember him stepping on my feet and swearing he's going to outlaw dancing the moment he becomes king.

Ronin's face is pleasant as he hums a low tune, lightening the tension as only the sophisticated know how. He turns us in slow circles, though I can tell he's still deep in thought.

"Whataya know, I guess I can dance." Surprise comes out in my tone, and if we weren't tiptoeing on tenterhooks, I'm sure I'd enjoy the thrill of doing something just for fun.

"Who are your parents, darling? How did you land in Neutral Territory?"

"Why, King Ronin Karamathian, you wouldn't be trying to distract me with a dance to coax personal information from me, would you?"

His eyes narrow as the pace of our footwork steps up. "You might think I want to know these things because I'm controlling or because I relish driving myself mad."

"I do love a good drive."

His mouth twitches. "I want to know what you're walking into. Will you be well-received? Will you show up there and be banished? This plan of ours will do little good if you get there and are kicked back into Neutral Territory straightaway. I know the fae are too delicate for capital punishment, which is the only thought that's allowed me some rest."

The wrinkle between his eyebrows is genuine—I've told enough lies in my life to spot the truth easily enough. "You're truly worried about me."

"Is that really so strange?"

"It's not normal for a vampire to care what happens to a fae."

"I prefer not to curse myself with the burden of being common."

I snigger. "You sound like an entitled prick when you talk like that."

He tsks as he turns me under his arm and then guides me back into the box step. "I'm not sure you're allowed to use words like 'entitled prick' during a waltz."

"Thanks for the tip. When I meet my new father-in-law, I'll be sure to leave that out." I drop his hands and step back, casting up a small smile for the gift of the dance. "I should get going. The more travel we can do in the daylight, the better."

Ronin catches my wrist as I pass him. He meets my eyes with concern. "You'll stay away from the Stone Graveyard. You will come back to me, yes?"

Des gets to see my bruised side. I don't talk about it, and I'm not even sure he knows what he's seeing, but there are moments when my smile can't be faked, and I let him have those moments. I don't want to give one to Ronin, but it slips out anyway. My smile dissolves and my snark quiets as a portion of the truth bubbles out of my lips before I can stop it. "I truly hope so."

With quick and strong hands he cups my face, tipping my chin up so he can examine the things I'm not ready for anyone to see. "You're terrified. What aren't you telling me?"

I lightly shove him away. "Afraid of the fae? I can't imagine anything sillier."

I want to tell him everything, to confess the awful man my father is. I want to throw my arms around Ronin's neck and sob for the horrors I've had to endure. I want to beg him not to let me go into the lion's den. I know how the fae are. They are worse than the vampires because the fae will smile to your face, then slowly comment, inserting small cuts in your armor until you're no bigger than a messy pile of bones. At least the vampires are forthcoming about their hatred. I can respect that. That's why I don't get too bent out of shape when Melinda comes after me. At least her hatred is genuine.

Instead of telling Ronin any more truth, I slap what I hope looks like bravery on my face and squeeze his hand twice to let him know that even though I have to put my scared self away and be bold right now, I'm still in here, screaming and sobbing and clawing at the walls of my psyche.

Then I let go of him and walk away before my feet betray me and keep me inside the fortress I've grown to love.

3

LIFE IN THE IVORUM PALACE

ALEXAVIER

I'm wearing my white military jacket, though honestly, it's only because it makes me look the part of a royal. I only served one term, and General Klein didn't allow me to do any fighting, no doubt on my parents' orders. What Salem does is real military work. I'm more the model for the uniform. "She should be here by now. Shouldn't she have come? It's going to be daylight soon."

My mother laughs, sitting on the balcony where I've been pacing for the past hour. "Alexavier, your fiancée will come. I can't wait to meet her. You've told me so little, I admit, I'm half-convinced she's imaginary."

"She's got a scar on her cheek. It's quite vicious. From an animal attack. So when you see her, don't mention it."

"You already told us as much. Honestly, it's like you think we're incapable of making a good first impression. She'll be lovely, I'm—"

The interruption is expected. After all, Mother's uttered a few sentences. "Far better than that dreadful girl you brought home last year. What was her name? Useless? Ufer?" Father sifts through documents I told him to look through last week, and he's only just getting to them after my fifth reminder.

"Eunice," I mutter. Father only talks freely around me, but sometimes I wish his words were filtered through some sieve of kindness. "You know her name. And don't do that with Lily. That whittling away at her self-confidence thing. You know how it irks me. You'll be polite and kind, because that's what your future daughter-in-law deserves."

Father frowns as he studies a line on the parchment I can tell he doesn't like. It's no doubt the same one I came across, indicating that we didn't send the amount of blood shipments to Drexdenberg that we charged them for. "It's so strange to me still that you're this taken with a woman after only a handful of months. Do you even know anything real about her?"

The landscape is all soaring trees broken up by ivorum-spike towers that glisten when the sun hits them just so. I grip the ivorum railing as a carriage comes near the palace through the tall, spindly trees, but then turns left. My shoulders slump. "I know she's for me, which is all you need to know. You both wanted me to choose a bride so I didn't have to rule alone someday, and I've chosen. The bloodline is secure. The kingdom shall have its princess, who will one day be queen of Faveda." *Among other things.*

"That's if I approve," Father says while Mother quiets.

She's always quiet when I need her to speak in my defense. Then again, she hasn't spoken up for herself in years. Not sure she sees a point in going up against Father, determined as he is to be the Alpha male in every room he enters.

I scoff at the veiled threat. "It's Lily or no one. You get to choose how long our bloodline lasts."

"Is that a threat?" He puts his hand on his broad chest, gasping like a true actor, but it's Mother who was the actress before father married her. Politics is the flipside of the acting coin—a currency Father uses to its maximum when he belittles her and then parades her around to the people as if she's the love of his life. Mother pretends like she loves him well enough.

Her unwrinkled silk dress goes an inch above her heels, making her long body and long face that much more noticeable. "Your father doesn't take kindly to being challenged. You know it's easiest to obey."

I cast her half a smile. "Yes, Father, you've taught me the art of getting one's way well enough. I will marry her, you will adore her, you will be civil, and I'll hear nothing more on the subject." My eyes scan the horizon, picking out a carriage here and there. It keeps getting my hopes up. What is taking them so long?

Mother stands up next to me at the edge of the balcony, casting her gleaming smile on the villagers who wave at her from below. She puts her fingers to her lips and then waves at them, as if she's blown a kiss. But she never does. It's always faked, this connection she claims to feel for the people. The truth is, she's isolated in the palace tower, not connected to much of anything or anyone. She kisses father like that too, and it irks me every time. Though, that much I understand. He treats her terribly, always speaking over her when she dares to speak in his presence at all, and talking down to her, as if she's too stupid to understand normal things.

Whatever. Not my marriage. Not my problem. Let them fake their kisses and their affection for the public. Fine by me.

Lily kisses me like I'm the thing helping her draw breath. I'll be damned if we end up air-smooching like Mother and Father do for the public now, moments before shooting snide comments under their breath at each other.

My eyes catch on Salem running through the marketplace in his enormous gray wolf form. My grin can't be helped when the fae scatter, afraid of getting too near the "filthy" shifter. Everything is lined in white down the main thoroughfare, and most of the people are wearing the traditional spotless, colorless clothes my kin are known for. Seeing dark blue jeans on Lily was the best kind of scandal.

Father's upper lip curls when he notices Salem heading in our direction. "Why doesn't he use a carriage? He's only upsetting everyone, prowling around Faveda out in the open like that. It's vulgar."

"Vulgar? Wow. I didn't know it was possible to run vulgarly. I'll be sure to tell him to run like a proper gentleman."

"Don't waste your breath on the brute. Keep him out of the dining room. It's no wonder he's never found a mate. A man of his age," Father scolds.

Mother comes to his aid, though I never understand why she bothers. "You know how dirt stains in the palace upset your father."

Father circles something on the page. "I swear, you'd think Prince Salem was trying to muddy up the place."

Well, he is.

I wave wildly enough to garner a nod from Salem as he runs toward the palace. I'm grinning like a little boy that I finally have an ally. My feet are quick as I run down the steps, offering up what I hope is a friendly nod at the guards in charge of the front gates. They never give Salem any trouble—he is a prince, after all—but Salem doesn't like to deal with them any more than they like to see his face on our land, so I fling open the front doors and welcome my friend with a hearty, "Prince Salem, how good it is to have you here. The guards were just readying to bow. Don't hold back, now. Go on."

They hate it when I do that. Makes me laugh every time.

I clap Salem on the back a few times before ushering him inside past the line of bowing soldiers. He doesn't want to deal with my parents, so we head to my room, which is in its own wing of the ivorum palace that sparkles like a pearl in the sunlight. Pays to be an only child, I guess.

The second we're alone, he shifts onto two legs, smoothing his gray hair out of his eyes. He refuses to look at me, no doubt because he doesn't want to see me gaping at his getup.

Salem wears exactly one outfit, and it never changes. Jeans, combat boots and his olive-green military shirt over a black undershirt. In battle, occasionally he'll wear his jacket, but only if his brother makes him. His chin-length gray hair is always a little greasy, but that's typical shifter hygiene, which is only compounded by the fact that the whole of Jacoba has been suffering a drought for far too long.

I can barely find words as he stands before me in his usual jeans and boots, paired with a light blue cowl neck sweater. The knitted thing looks like it belongs on a man who smokes a pipe and comments on the finer things in life, which has never been Salem, who doesn't prefer to comment on much of anything. His hair has been recently washed and cut short, buzzed in back with only two inches of spiky gray on top. There isn't the usual five days' worth of crud under his fingernails. "Salem, what... You look... It's..."

He never turns the full brunt of his snarl on me, but his upper lip begins to curl as his hackles raise. "I wouldn't go finishing those sentences if ye know what's good for ye."

I cross my arms and then press my finger to my lower lip. "I can't believe you let a barber near you. Does he still have his hands?"

Worry flashes in his slate eyes. "It looks bad?"

"No! No, it looks fantastic. I'm just trying to wrap my mind around the total transformation. Did Justice make you do this for some reason?" Then the truth dawns on me, bringing a grin to my lips that firms up Salem's scowl. "Ah. You cut your hair to look nice for Lily."

"Shut your gob about it. I knew I looked ridiculous." He moves to pull off his sweater, and I see he's wearing his olive military shirt beneath, just in case.

"Wait! I didn't mean anything bad by it. Just an observation. Lily will love it."

He doesn't believe me, so he turns back into his bear-sized wolf, which I notice now has slightly shorter gray fur.

I shake my head at him. "You, my dearest friend, are a coward. Face a whole battalion by yourself, no problem, but put you in front of little Lily, and you're a mess."

He growls at me, but that seems to be the most he's willing to continue conversing about the subject. His ears perk up, and I know he's hearing something I should've been listening for. We race down the stairs together, occasionally shoving each other out of the way, as we did when we were teenagers racing to dinner while our parents argued over boundary lines and borders in the study.

The guards are helping Des out of the carriage, but he casts me a look of mild frustration that all is not well. "Brothers, it's good to see you. Have I got a grand surprise for you both."

I frown and trot forward, shooing Des inside, since there's only twenty minutes or so left of the moonlight. "Go on up to my room. The shades are drawn and the windows boarded for you." Then to one of the guards, I say, "Prepare the hallways and the study on my floor for

Prince Destino. The sun will be up soon, so make sure the boards are over all the windows in the east wing. I think I got them all, but if you could double-check."

"Yes, your majesty." He bows to me, then gives a forced, curt bow to Des before trotting indoors. The constipated expression they all wear when they have to mind their political manners makes me chuckle every time.

"Before you overreact, she's fine," Des calls to me from inside the house.

"That's very reassuring." I step toward the carriage, but Salem is already darting inside, his howl of agony lighting my nerves on fire.

"Where are ye cut?" I hear him shout, so I know he's changed back into his man form.

I jump into the carriage, my mouth falling open at the sight of my fiancée covered in blood.

4

BLOODY WAITRESS

SALEM

I'm the one asking her questions, but I can't focus enough to hear her answers. Blood. So much blood. On her neck, in her hair, down her arms and covering her thermal t-shirt. She's injured in too many places, yet she's looking at me like I'm overreacting. "Show me where!"

I'm shouting at her. I don't mean to be, but seeing her like this takes away my ability to think about things like whether or not I'm scaring her.

Of course I'm scaring her.

"You cut your hair!" she finally answers.

I stop to gape at her. "Tha's all ye can think about right now? You're bleeding out!"

"No, it's not all mine. We had a little accident on the way in. Then a little incident. I was hoping not to make a big scene, but maybe that's blown now, what with all the yelling. Is there like, a back entrance or something?"

The horse's reins feed in through a slit in the front of the carriage, so vampires can direct them without a driver in the sunlight if need be. The front flap lifts so they can see out a tinted screen. Alex is together enough to do as she asks, and drives us around the palace toward the back, which butts up to the ocean. Leave it to the fae to block one of nature's beauties with a stinking display of their wealth. The palace cuts the view of the ocean, but the fae all love it. The sun will rise on the water in minutes, but I can't bring myself to enjoy any of it.

"Tell me where you're hurt," I finally manage to say at a volume tha doesn't spook her.

"Prince Salem, I'm really okay."

Prince Salem. She doesn't use Des' title, and even calls him by his shortened name. She has a cutesy nickname for Alex. But I've known her for years, and I'm still Prince Salem.

I frown at a tear in her jeans where an angry cut is clearly visible along her right thigh. "Ye were in a knife fight." I've seen enough to know what I'm looking at.

She grimaces, and then juts her chin out. "If you're looking for an apology, I didn't start it."

Jays, she's beautiful, bloodstains and all.

"I'm looking only to make sure you're alright. I don't care about getting ye in trouble. I only care if *you're in trouble.*"

Her eyebrows lift, as if I've said something shocking. "Well, thank you. It's really no big deal. Could've been a lot worse."

"No big deal? You're my…" My reason for being here? My love? "You're my waitress," I finish lamely, grimacing at how trite tha sounds.

The carriage comes to a stop and Alex grabs her bags before he hops down, holding the door open for us with his foot.

I don't ask, and I don't have it in me to care about her pride as I tuck one arm behind her back and the other under her thighs, lifting her in my arms as I step from the carriage.

I'm holding her. I'm holding Lily. She's a feather in my arms, so I take great care not to jostle her.

"You don't have to… Honestly, I'm fine."

"I don't care if ye don't want me carrying ye. You're injured and bloody all over. Just let me do this."

Her mouth draws to the side, but she doesn't protest further. I'm learning the only time I can ignore her wishes is when she's injured. The need to take care of her is stronger than my desire to give in to whatever she wants.

This woman has always been a danger to me, but I taunt myself regularly, going back to her pub over and over to be near the thing I shouldn't touch.

And now she's in my arms. Her face is buried in my shoulder as I take her inside. I know it's because she's embarrassed and doesn't want to be seen, not because she actually wants me near her. But I pretend tha's what this is, tha she's my girlfriend, maybe even my wife, to look after when she falls to disrepair. I pretend she trusts me to be her safe place, and my chest swells at the lie I love.

No one's actually in this part of the palace, so I take her upstairs to Alex's room, because at this point, I realize maybe she is more embarrassed than injured. Alex plops down the bags and leans on the wall next to Des, after he locks the door behind us so we can get the whole story.

Alex's room is fancy, with lace on the curtains and gold and ivorum glinting off every surface beneath the glow of the ornate crystal light fixture overhead. It's too much, I've always thought, but Lily's special enough to deserve a room tha's too much.

I should set her down on the bed, but I can't lay her on the mattress she'll share with another man. I just can't. So I kick at the ivorum chair, turning the pearly white thing toward the guys so we can all see her as I lower her onto the seat.

Alex puts to words the panic I can't brush aside, no matter how casual she's acting. "Care to explain how you came to us so damaged?"

5

SIMPLE TOUCHES

SALEM

I should give Lily some space, go stand next to the lads, but I can't bring myself to part from her when she might be in pain. I finally manage to march into the bathroom and pull out a washrag, so at least I can clear off some of this blood. Then I'll know what we're dealing with. Des offers to tend to her, but I grip the wet rag tighter because I'm a selfish man and want an excuse to be near her a little bit longer. It's no chore to kneel before her. I need to look at her leg, get to the source of the problem, but I'm not sure if I'm allowed to touch her thigh. She leans forward, her breath coming in small bursts across the nape of my neck, toying with parts of me usually left untouched.

How I want her to touch me. Anywhere. Everywhere. I wish life were different, tha someone this incredible could want me.

Des explains in a low voice meant to ease the tension.

"We traveled through Neutral Territory so I could bring gifts to Fiora from King Ronin, and so Lily could see her mum. Fiora was in the middle of treating someone who was bleeding out, so Lily helped. That's where most of the blood came from. Then after we washed up, changed our clothes and had a bite to eat, we wanted to beat the sunrise, so we left in the carriage. On our way into Faveda, the carriage was attacked because it's clearly mine. Lily gets a little vicious when she's scared."

Indignation cracks out of her like a whip. "I wasn't scared for me. I was scared I'd be pulling another arrow out of you! Does nobody understand that Des is it for the Drexdenberg monarchy? That if he dies, there goes the ruling family?"

Des quirks his eyebrow, waiting for the truth to dawn on her. "Actually, if I died, the throne would go to you. That's kind of the whole point of our little shtick here."

Her whole body tightens, and I can practically feel dozens of arguments roiling through her, filtering through the logic of Des' words. She knows this. We've told her this.

She swallows down her frustration with a firm, "I don't like when you're snatched at. That feeling should be common among all Drexdenberg residents, which I am. I don't protect you just because you're useful or because I love you so much. You're also my prince."

Des has bags under his eyes, but he smiles at her declaration. "You're such a soft one. I'm alright, blue eyes. Barely a scratch on me, thanks to you. Cheers."

Alex clamps his hand down on my shoulder. "Are you going to clean off the blood, Salem?"

"Aye. Don't rush me."

Her eyes flicker with something tha looks like she thinks I just called her ugly or something. I don't understand it.

I can't touch her thigh. I just can't. She doesn't want me to, and I want it too badly. So I wipe the dried blood off her wrists and hands, which she doesn't seem to mind.

I love every part of this. She smells like lilies, peaches and the earth, beneath the stink of blood. Of all the times I sat at the bar, I never dreamed I'd get this lucky. We're almost holding hands.

Alex frowns at just how much dried blood is caked on her skin. "Lily-girl, you can clean up in my bathroom, alright? I'll lay out fresh clothes for you. Wash the long ride off yourself."

Her attention flits to Des. "You go first. I know you're exhausted."

"Are you certain?"

"No, so I'd take the offer and run with it before I change my mind."

Des chuckles, and I can hear the long journey in the slow staccato of the sound.

Tha means I get to keep mopping the grime off her, which suits me just fine. The lantern light flickers off Alex's knowing expression, and though we're here for her to marry him, he casts me a wry grin because he knows just how much this means to me. "I'll go see about bringing up some food. You hungry?"

"Only starving," she admits.

Des closes himself in the washroom and Alex leaves for the kitchen, and finally, it's just the two of us. Her breath slows, hitting my neck at just the right angle to inflict pure torture. I'm no good at small talk, but I do my best impersonation of a lad who is. "Long ride?"

She nods. If she wants to inch away, she doesn't make any move toward the door. "How do you do it?" she finally asks in a quiet voice.

"Do what?"

"Care about them so much? I was a nervous wreck, worried Des would get shot again. I'm not used to this. It's always been just Fiora and me, and almost everyone knows better than to mess with her. And they stay away from me because they know my dagger has silver in it."

"Carrying a silver blade is truly testing the limits of your diplomatic immunity. Remember tha when ye travel to Jacoba. Silver kills vampires, sure, but it can weaken the magic of shifters when we touch it, so it's not something we tolerate on our land either."

She shrugs. "I only stab people who ask for it."

"How many on your way here?"

She swallows hard, so I know it affects her to take a life. Still, she holds her chin high, trying to convince me she doesn't care. "Only three."

I shake my head at her, clucking my tongue. "Now you've done it. You're robbing me of decorating my prison with more lowlifes." Then I wipe aside all teasing. "No more, aye? This isn't Neutral Territory. If ye want to be a true Territorial, ye can't go solving every problem by killing off an immortal."

She casts me a look of disbelief. "Let's just agree to disagree on that one." Then her face sobers. "How do you care so much about Des and Lexi like this? The smallest inconvenience they might come up against hits me harder than it should. I mean, they're grown men."

I love her. If there's a truer thing than tha, I don't know it. She loves my friends and cares if they come to ruin. Not much else speaks to my heart louder than tha. It's then I decide to let her in on a little secret. "Count your heartbeats. Ye know, when you're being attacked. Don't count them as they are, but as ye want them to be. Then your racing heart will slow to the pace your mind sets. Far easier to fight tha way, rather than going for the kill and ending a life. Ye can be more strategic tha way."

"Huh?"

It's a bold move, but I'm just reckless enough to try it. I take her free hand I've freshly scrubbed, and press it to my heart. I count out the beats in a whisper. "One, two, three, four… Just like tha. When I'm in a fight, I count slower, and try to get my licks in between the heartbeats. Then I don't lose myself to panic, and I can see the whole scene clearer. Less overwhelming."

Her hand stays over my heart, just like how she does with Des. Like her hand wants to touch some part of me tha exists only for her. "I've never seen you in a sweater before. This is so soft."

It's not what I'm expecting her to say, but I'll take it.

She rubs in a circle, but her palm remains over my heart. I'm suddenly a fan of sweaters. "Prince Salem?" she whispers.

"Salem," I finally correct her. It's been years I've been wanting her to drop my title. Maybe it's having her so close and all to myself tha's loosening my tongue, but suddenly I find I can ask for a portion of what I want. "I've known ye for five years, Hannah," I tease, using the false name she gave so long ago. "Ye don't need to use my stuffy title. Just Salem."

She fingers my collar, her thumb brushing my throat. I can't believe my good fortune. She's all soft and feminine with gentle curves and all the right smells.

I'm so captivated by her tha I barely catch the angst tha flashes in her eyes before her whole face mutates to worry. When she grips the fabric on my chest and balls it into a fist, she leans forward, like whatever she's afraid of needs to be kept secret. "I don't want to be here!"

I don't know what to say to tha, so I smooth my hand over her forearm, coaxing out more of her confessions. "Tell it to me," I urge her. "Tell it all."

"These are the people who didn't notice when an eight-year-old went missing. The General will know it's me, and he'll try to kill me again! The second we crossed over onto fae soil, this dread started growing in my stomach. I can't shake it. I don't belong here."

"But you're fae. This is exactly where ye belong."

With me. Ye belong with me. Though, as I think this, a mental image pops into my mind of Lily holding my hand as we walk through Jacoba together. She's all beautiful, young and clean, and I'm gritty, old and dirty. It's clear she doesn't belong with me.

Her breath near my neck is making me dizzy.

I swallow tha down and try to live in this moment, the one where she stays close, confesses her secrets, and doesn't try to flit away.

"I belong in Neutral Territory where no one expects me to be more than I am! I'm not a princess or a queen. I'm not someone who can stand back and watch while Des is... I can stab a vampire who attacks what's mine, but I've never had to defend myself against a fae before. That's what's going to happen if I stay here. General Klein is going to try to kill me off again. I can't kill a fae with a silver dagger! Silver does nothing to them!"

This is where I know I'm the man for her. A chuckle slips from my lips. "I can teach ye all ye need to know there. Fae are far easier than vampires. Too delicate for a stiff breeze, most of them."

"Can you teach me?"

The sound of Des' shower in the background nearly covers her words, but I hear them. I hear her asking for my help. It's not the same as actually wanting to spend time with me, but I pretend it is. "Of course. After ye get some sleep."

She looks so nervous; I'm worried she might throw up.

It's then I realize her arms are tightening until they're clasped around my neck, like a child afraid to let go. She leans forward and presses her forehead to mine. It's all I can hope tha my heart doesn't stop from having her so near. This can't be real, yet it is. I can feel her, smell her, hear her soft whisper when it finally comes just for me. "I don't want to sleep here. I can't. The General will come for me."

"Then I will come for him," I promise. Maybe women prefer things like flowers and candy instead of vows of vengeance, but I know she doesn't prefer those things to the gift of feeling safe. "If I stay here, will ye sleep?"

She snorts. "That might be the only way that happens."

My chest swells with pride as I pretend it's me she wants for more than just muscle. "Then I'll stay."

Forever. As long as it takes.

This seems to be the right thing to say, because she settles contentedly as she hugs me just like tha, sighing her sweet seduction against my skin. My lips are three inches from hers, but they know not to dream of something as grand as kissing her.

After a few beats, her fingers tease the freshly-shaved hairs lining the nape of my neck. My eyes close, and I wonder if there's ever been a luckier lad than me.

6

———————

WHITE SILK

LILYA

I'm nervous, and can't remember the simplest thing. I knocked over my glass of water Lexi brought up for me, and can't stop apologizing. At least Salem didn't catch my clumsy moment. "This isn't going to work! I can't... I don't know how to... I don't belong here!" My words come out in a desperate plea for any of them to somehow keep this from happening. I knew I wouldn't be able to luck into marrying all three of them in secret, but part of me hoped that might be the case. I don't want to do the meeting-the-parents thing. I don't want any of it. My father's barking disapproval before every social event I was expected to attend comes screaming back to me with every move I make. I'm not sitting straight enough. My chin isn't level to the floor. My teeth are grinding out my nerves, which is the exact opposite of the "lips together, teeth apart" mantra that was drilled into me from a young age.

I snag a towel from the bathroom and do what I can to

sop up the two inches of water that spilled from my cup onto the carpet. I've not had carpet in my adolescent or adult life, so I have no idea if clear liquid can stain the pure white fibers.

Lexi picks up the pearl-colored cup and sets it on my empty lunch tray. "It's all fine. You're worried about nothing. After standing up to the whole of Drexdenberg, I'm surprised being announced to your own people is the thing that's tipped it all. No one's going to protest you here with picket signs and calls for your removal."

I lift my chin, the rag stilling what little cleaning it's doing. My eyes go dead along with all the cheeriness I can fake when I tell him, "The fae are not my people. Fiora is my people. You three are my people. Ronin is my people. The list ends there."

Des and Lexi still for a few beats, until finally Des breaks the silence. "We're not going to leave you to face the fae by yourself if it all goes south, yeah? If you don't want to do this, you don't have to. We've made a good enough statement with our marriage. If we want to leave the plan at that, it's still a big step in the right direction."

Lexi's body tenses, his eyes watching my most miniscule move. My gaze falls to the water spill. "I want to marry Lexi, whether or not it makes a political statement. It's the rest of the country that makes me nervous."

Lexi's shoulders relax in a gust from his lips. "That's good to know. I feel the same way, Lily-girl. We'll get through this. Compared to Drexdenberg, this'll be a piece of cake."

"Until they find out that I'm also Des' wife. That part's going to be harder for them to swallow."

When Salem comes out of the bathroom, his eyes widen in time with the shout bursting from his lips. "Ye don't kneel on the floor!" He crosses the room in three long strides and snatches the rag from my fist. He pries me off the carpet and descends to his knees with a firm frown, swiping at the wet spot. "Ye don't clean carpeting. You're a princess. One day you'll be the Queen of Jacoba. Made me sick to my stomach to watch ye mopping up spills at the pub. You're not starting out this portion of your life on your knees."

It's the meanest his tone has ever sounded at me, and the nicest thing he's ever said. I can't help myself—my arms around his shoulders before I got some sleep when we first arrived must've set something loose. Before I can talk sense into my brain, I lean down and throw my arms around his neck, hoping he doesn't shrug me away.

He stills, and I know it's because I'm fae and I'm not supposed to do things like this with a shifter. Despite the fact that he let me give him an almost-hug this morning, he's still been raised to think I'm trying to trick him at every turn.

Instantly, a wave of chagrin rolls through me. He's not hugging me in return, and he didn't participate in the almost-hug this morning either. I let my imagination run away with me. I was so tired and stressed and spent that I thought about what I wanted, and not what he's made clear I can never have.

My arms loosen and begin to slide off his shoulders as mortification paints my cheeks. But they cling once more when Salem drops the rag, coils an arm around my hips and stands, lifting me nearly a foot off the ground. My legs are dangling as I hang onto him, but I've never felt more secure. He doesn't say a word as his gray eyes burn me with too many things I'll never understand about him. I feel his heartbeat touching my skin, warming me in this tropical place that feels so very cold.

It's my one chance. He's so close, and this time he's looking right at me. Too many times I've dreamed of kissing this beautiful man. His lips are full, sculpted with the arches taunting me, telling me to come close, but stay far away.

Instead of taking what I've always wanted, I test my daring by kissing his cheek. Though he was freshly shaved a few hours ago, his scruff bristles against my lips. The smell of his face is a fresh hit of sawed oak. He's the woods incarnate, and I'm lucky enough to have my arms around him, and his around me.

"Easy," he breathes, his voice rough. He releases me so I slide down his body. His hand touches his cheek, his eyes wide in shock as he stares at me.

I know what he's thinking. He can't believe a fae would get so carried away that a kindness turned into something more in her mind. I'm horrified that I kissed his cheek, and in front of the guys, no less. My eyes dart to the bed, where a white gown I've been too nervous to touch practically glows atop the lace coverlet.

I scurry away from Salem and grab up the dress. "I'll get changed, and we can go meet your parents," I call to Lexi, keeping my reddening face away from all three of them.

I shut myself in the bathroom, reminding myself that I already know Lexi's parents. His mother used to put my hair in pigtails, claiming the General had no idea what he was doing. King Fairbucks used to keep peppermints in his pocket for me. Every time he'd hand me one, he would smile and shake his finger at me, warning me that sugar made little girls into fat women who died alone.

And the fae wonder why they're hated by the rest of the world.

They won't recognize me. I've been dead for sixteen years. Lilya is one of the most common fae names.

I try to calm myself with useless pep talks to avoid owning up to kissing Salem's cheek. He shouldn't hold me like that. Shouldn't smell so damn good. I have to stay away from him, or I'll end up making him really uncomfortable.

I quickly strip and then wash my hands and face, checking to make sure I'm perfectly clean all over before sliding the white silk over my body. It feels like water on my skin, and a little like a lie. I don't belong in spotless clothes that announce to the world I'm a fine woman of distinction. I belong in something I can wear that won't be a bother if I get ale spilled on it.

This thing is… Is it pretty? Is it sexy? Is it an undergarment? I can't tell. The strappy top isn't so low cut that I'm afraid I'll spill out of it, but it definitely doesn't make any effort to hide that I'm a woman. The seductive material falls to just below my knees. The back of this gown is… well, I can't wear a bra, that's for sure. The V between my shoulders dips down past the midpoint of my spine, so I make sure to wear my lavender curls down to cover most of it.

I can't look at myself for more than three seconds before the sight hurts my eyes. But this is the job. This is my costume I'm to wear to play the role of the fae bride I'll soon be. When I slip out of the bathroom, the guys are talking in hushed tones that quiet the second I join them.

Salem takes a step back, his eyes looking everywhere but at me. Des grins and reaches out to loop his littlest finger through mine. It's the perfect way to steal away a portion of my nerves. I'm not sure Des realizes how right he is for me, even when we're all wrong for each other. Without letting go of my finger, he brings me in for a hug that's so loving, I want to live in his arms forever. I'm still me in this dress, and we're still us. He's not afraid to touch me, so in turn, I remind myself not to be so frightened of the very fae way I now look. It's not safety Des gives me, but love. I feel the truth of it in everything he does, every brush of his skin against mine. We've slept only three hours, but he feigns relaxation for the sake of me not tipping over the edge of reason. "This is the easy part," he promises.

And the thing about Des is I know he truly believes that. He might be wrong, but he's so sure of me and this whole plan, and his belief that one day things will be better for all of us, that his optimism leaks onto me. My spirit lifts a marginal amount, which allows me to relax into his half-embrace.

When I turn to Lexi, there's a tenderness in his gaze. "You're fae," he comments, as if it's some revelation.

"I've always been fae."

"But the dress. You look like us. Like the woman I'm going to marry." Lexi's shoulders roll back, and a calm smile lifts the corners of his mouth. "They're waiting for us, Lily-girl. This is the meet-the-parents part where I tell them I'm in love with you, and they greet the daughter they've always wanted."

I run my hand down the front of my dress. "They won't know it's me, thank goodness."

"Maybe they should."

I quirk an eyebrow at Lexi. "They definitely should not. It'll be shocking enough when they learn about my marriage to Des. If the General learns that I'm still alive? That the woman marrying the fae prince is his daughter who's supposed to be dead? It'll be trouble, Lexi."

There's a challenge to my logic in Lexi's eyes but he smooths it over. "Whatever you like."

I'm dubious about the seamlessness of it all, but I don't argue aloud. "One problem before we go. I don't have a place to strap my dagger. Can't exactly conceal a weapon in this dress."

Salem's lips pucker into a frown. "Ye don't need to fight if I'm around. What trouble do ye imagine will fall on ye at a fae dinner?"

I want to tell him that fae are capable of just as much

treachery; they just don't like to get their hands dirty with it. But I decide to trust Salem, since I have no other option. I drop Des' finger and take Lexi's proffered arm, walking with him through the hallways and down the staircase.

I'm seeing more of the palace now, taking in the details I breezed by when Salem carried me up to hide out in Lexi's room. So many things are totally new, yet key details call out to me as if I never left them behind.

"We tied ropes just here," I say to Lexi, stopping to loop my finger around one of the spokes in the banister along the too many stairs. The wealthier fae like tall ceilings, so what could be a five-story palace really has only two levels with ridiculously high ceilings. It makes going up and down the stairs a real chore when your legs are too short to accomplish much.

Lexi tilts his head at me. "What's that?"

I crouch down, probably wrinkling my dress, and Lexi mimics my body language while the guys stand behind us. "We tied ropes here and climbed down the walls. Thought it would be faster than all these steps. But it took us twice as long to pull ourselves up. We got in so much trouble when the General saw us."

Lexi's smile is genuine. Why would anyone ever call him a tricky fae? "That's right. You were supposed to be in elocution lessons while I was supposed to be studying. Father sent me to bed without dessert that night."

My eyes fix on the ivorum banister, seeing it not as it is now, but as it was so many years ago. "The General took a switch to me. Then he cut the head off one of my dolls and set the body on fire. Told me if I ever skipped my lessons again, he'd do that to the rest of them."

Lexi's mouth pulls in a grimace. "Please tell me you're joking. That's sick."

I lean into Lexi's body, breathing while my ribs will still allow movement. I know well the feeling of suffocation when all the life and love are sucked out of a room by the subtle needling of fae politics. "No one beats me now," I say like a promise to myself. "No one burns my treasures. You're my treasures, you know," I tell the guys.

Lexi's arm bands around me as he kisses me behind my ear. "And you're mine. My very own." His lips tickle my skin with a whisper. "One day, this palace will be ours. If you see something that offends you or brings back painful recollections, I'll have it removed. Only the bad memories will be the things that burn before your eyes, not your treasures. I will make this place good for you, Lily-girl. I love you."

The angle is awkward when I turn my chin to kiss him, but it's worth it. His lips are soft, given to smiling often, and promising me beautiful things. I can't not kiss him. My fingers brush against the softness of his shaved cheek, coaxing a luscious noise of contentment that vibrates from deep in his chest.

"I love you, too," I remind him when I rest my forehead to his.

"I'll take care of this. Trust me to make this place good for you."

I don't see how that's possible, but I nod anyway,

because I trust that Lexi will do all he can to make this work. He helps me up, brushes a crease out of my thin-strapped dress, and kisses my bare shoulder before escorting me the rest of the way.

Salem's back to giving me enough space to fit an elephant between us, which I know means my hug absolutely ruined everything.

I'm not allowed in the receiving room. That's for important grown-up talk when foreign officials visit. My spine angles away, but the rest of me follows where Lexi leads.

King Fairbucks is standing by the window, peering out the side of the closed curtains. Though it's been sixteen years, not much has changed about him, except that he's collected a few extra crinkles around the corners of his eyes, and his belly's gone a bit soft. He's got perfectly-trimmed white-blond hair, just like Lexi's, but his is veering more towards white than blond. The king is wearing his white suit jacket over a spotless shirt and matching pants. He's so bright, he almost looks like he's glowing.

Queen Kloe Fairbucks sits in her ivorum chair, one leg crossed over the other, martini in hand. Her silk dress is tight and long, her blonde curls pinned around her ears to showcase her swan-like neck. She smiles in our direction, and a million memories flood my mind of her looking exactly like this—sexy white dress, martini in hand, and a welcoming smile that stays brightly lit even when everyone around her is saying nasty things.

They don't know me. I don't know them. I'm some random fae chick Lexi happened to meet when…

We don't have a story. We don't have any believable lie we've agreed upon to conjure up for the parents. Panic wells up in me through my forced smile, making my nails dig deeper into Lexi's forearm as I curtsy, dipping my head in respect of the throne before uttering anything that might come out in a pathetic bleat.

King Fairbucks beams at us. "Ah! Finally, we meet the girl we've heard so much about. So much and so little, really. Alexavier's told us all about his love for you, how amazing you are, how beautiful, but hardly anything about who you are. Come sit. You must tell us everything."

King Fairbucks motions to the chaise lounge while Queen Kloe smiles with her mouth but not her eyes. "Yes, you'll have to take some of the mystery out of the equation for us. Just who are you? Alexavier wouldn't even give us your name."

I open my mouth as I sit next to Lexi on the expertly upholstered ivorum chaise lounge, but the fae prince answers for me while Des and Salem flank our seat like guards. "Actually mother, you already know her."

My spine stiffens and my head jerks toward Lexi.

Without a pause, without a stutter, and without my consent, Lexi says, "This is Lilya Klein, General Klein's deceased daughter."

7

MEETING THE PARENTS

ALEXAVIER

*L*ily never would've gone along with my parents knowing who she is, but Father's too cunning not to sniff out a secret and dig until he hits the bottom. *I* want to be the one controlling her story, not him. Watching her cling to Salem sealed it for me. I can't stomach her being afraid in her homeland, in my house. She's used to having no power, to being told where to go and how to be. She doesn't know how much sway she holds now with my title in her grasp.

She's white as a sheet, horror twisting her previously plastered-on smile no one was buying as sincere. I don't know what the big deal is; it's not like she did anything wrong to earn the General's monstrous behavior. This must come out, and this way, we control the narrative.

"Close the doors," Father orders, snapping his fingers at Salem. It's a game they play, where he orders Salem around like a dog, and Salem doesn't obey. I don't know what they both get out of it, but it's been going on for as long as I can remember.

"No," I rule. "Everyone will hear of it soon enough. No sense in keeping it a secret now. General Klein took his daughter and dropped her in shifter territory to get rid of her, hoping the wild animals would kill her off. She escaped, barely eight years old, and wandered into Neutral Territory, where she's been living ever since."

Mother's glass clatters sloppily on the stand beside her, her horrified expression sincere. I've been reading lies on that woman my whole life, so I know she had nothing to do with Lily's almost-death. "That's not true! General Klein would never do something so cruel!"

Father pinches the bridge of his nose. "Stop squawking, Kloe. I can barely think."

My mother snaps her mouth shut, and I hate the sight of the immediate obedience.

Father takes Lily's hand, not quite jerking her up, but his hold is forceful enough that she complies, stumbling where he leads. "Stand back, Destino. I need better light." Though we're the only territory with electricity, due to the magic fae naturally give off, the bulbs are often a point of pride and not nearly as efficient as natural light. Father flings open the curtain furthest away, but Salem still moves to block Des from the light that'll never stretch far enough to touch him. In the sunbeams that filter in through the window, Lily seems to shine like she's made of pure light.

Father's neck muscles are tensed, the vein in his forehead throbbing as it always does when something happens outside of his control. "Is this true?" he asks her.

I throw my hands up. "Of course it's true! You can see it's her. Picture our Lily-girl running around in pigtails and lacy dresses, then add sixteen years. It's her!"

"Silence!" Father shouts, his authoritarian voice filling the room so much that Lily jumps.

She's trembling, and when she steps out of the near-blinding light, my chest tightens when I catch the sight of tears streaming down her cheeks. In all of the many changes, I don't think she's cried. She's moved, left her maternal guardian, been hated by an entire people, and been attacked multiple times, but I haven't seen her cry about any of it yet.

"Is it true, girl?" When Father's hands grip her biceps so hard a squeak belts out of her, I shout for him to let her go.

Salem pushes Des down behind the white lounger and beelines for the two. "No one puts their hands on her, not even kings who should know better." He rips Lily from my father, shielding her with his massive form.

Father stiffens. "I needed to see her in the light and she was trying to scurry away. Lies are easier away from the sun, and this is no time for trickery."

"I gave ye a warning because you're Alex's da. Next time ye grab her, my knife comes out."

Salem's never threatened my family before. Then again, he's never been in love before Lily came along.

Father takes note of the change and nods once. "If she's telling the truth, I won't harm her. If she's lying, twisting my son's mind with poison against my most trusted official, she will pay most dearly, and not even your blade can stop that."

I get the feeling that even if somehow Lily wasn't telling the truth, Salem would still fight to the death in her honor.

"Girl, come into the light. Shadows are unbefitting a moment like this." Father snaps his fingers at her, and I cringe. My wife shouldn't be beckoned like an animal.

Still, she obeys, if only to keep Salem from spilling my father's blood on the white carpeting. The two stand with the window framing them, lighting them in a glow that looks otherworldly. This room is a place that tolerates a myriad of lies, but now demands nothing but the absolute truth.

"Tell me who you are and why I should believe you."

Her tears glisten as if each one has glimmers of pure silver in it, lighting from the sun's rays off her creamy skin. She's shaking like a leaf, and it's then I truly see how much fear she's been holding inside.

Maybe I shouldn't have told my parents without warning her I'd be doing so. She wanted to keep her past secret from them, play a game that could never hold water in the long run.

Does she not know that I love her? Does she not understand that we'll be married forever? She cannot be Hannah in one territory and Lilya in another.

The decision that seemed so very clear minutes ago now is muddled with murky clouds, making me wonder if telling them who she is was the right move. Judging by the tremble in her voice when she finally opens her mouth, perhaps I went wrong somewhere.

"I'm Lilya Klein. Lexi's telling the truth. I'm the General's daughter."

Father steps backward, his mouth open but no sound spilling out.

Mother stands on wobbling legs, tripping on her way to the window. She peers into Lily's eyes, seeking out lies I can tell she's praying are there. "A fae in Neutral Territory? It's not possible! Only filth lives there."

Lily's mostly bare back touches the window, literally cornered as she runs out of space to put between herself and my parents.

This is temporary. She charmed King Ronin so easily that those two count each other as being one of their few treasured people.

But these are actually her people. This is a rough patch, a necessary bump down the road to an infinitely smoother life. Someday soon, Father will call her his daughter, and Mother will greet her with a kiss. It's not as if any of this is Lily's fault.

I don't understand what I'm looking at when Mother grabs Lily by the head, forcing a shriek out of my fiancée when Mother bends Lily in half so she can leaf through the lavender tresses.

"I warned ye!" Salem rips Mother away from Lily and flings the Queen of Faveda toward the furthest wall. Des cusses loudly from his crouched position, having inched along the side of the lounger so he can watch the mayhem without going near the sun.

It's a tribute to how scandalized my parents are at Lily's unveiling that neither of them addresses Salem manhandling the matriarch. Honestly, I'm not sure Father cares, except for appearance's sake.

Mother points her finger in accusation at Lily. "Lilya Klein had a pink heart-shaped birthmark on the back of her head! Find it for me, and I'll believe it's really her. I need proof, more than just words. Fae lies are hardest to spot."

Salem gives Lily his arm to hold onto, since it looks like she might need something solid to steady herself. The sight of her leaning on him in my parents' home snaps me to action. I cross the room and grab her up in a bear hug meant to shield just as much as it's meant to comfort. But instead of melting into my body, as she usual does, my Lily-girl goes rigid, remaining in my arms but not savoring my touch. Then she makes a clear statement by gently but firmly pushing me away.

Des stands, motioning for her to go to him and escape my family.

Me. To escape *me.*

Salem shuts the curtain, dimming the room that's now lit only by two bulbed ivorum lamps. Lily runs to Des. Actually runs. She throws her arms around his neck and holds him so tight, his eyes bulge. His hands graze up and down her naked spine, calming her as I meant to have done. Another man is comforting my wife in my home. I'm not indignant or slighted; I'm ashamed.

Des presses his cheek to hers. "Can Salem look through your hair and find the birthmark? Would that be alright? No one's going to put their hands on you without your say-so."

She nods, her face buried in his shoulder.

Des motions Salem forward. His thick fingers fumble through her hair before he pulls aside enough so show the rest of the room what's been clear to me for quite some time: Lilya Klein is still very much alive.

"Get away from the vampire, dear," Father scolds her in a taut, strangled voice, clicking his fingers through his shock.

Lily doesn't obey, and that small victory gives me hope that she can stand in this world where people are going to constantly be telling her where to go and who she should be. Instead she clings tighter to Des, her left hand finding its way to his chest, as if he's her tether to truth.

"You died," Mother says, her words lingering in the center of the room. There's a clear divide now—my biological family on one side, and my true family clear across on the other. And I'm standing on the wrong side. "We scattered your ashes in the ocean behind the palace."

"Enough, Kloe," Father chastises with a bite in his voice. "No one needs to hear you mutter about this."

My mother goes silent, though it's clear she has questions brimming behind her painted lips.

Father takes over, as he often does. "You were one of the children who perished in the attack on the primary schools when the vampires wanted more blood than we agreed to."

Des' eyes go cold as he glares at my parents over Lily's shoulder. "The lie you were sold by General Klein cost my country a great many soldiers when you launched a counterattack to an assault we didn't do! That's the battle that started it all, and you still won't admit that you had no right to attack us! We would never target children."

"That's neither here nor there at this point." Father runs his hand over his face.

Des doesn't release Lily from his protective embrace. "While we're on the subject of Drexdenberg, it seems a few shipments of blood our people paid for have gone missing."

Father sighs and rolls his eyes. "Oh?"

He knows. I showed him as much, and when he required yet more proof and more, I dug it up for him, scouring the logs and standing beside him while he read the proof. It's then I realize that even though he knows all about it, he was counting on the vampires not wanting to interact with the fae, and skating over the issue.

"Des is being generous," I announce, my tongue sliding over my top row of teeth. "The fae are seventy-nine cases short of what we owe Drexdenberg. I can't imagine how such a mistake was made. I'll give the order to send over all we owe them, so we're up to date on the trade deal." When Father opens his mouth to protest, I hold up my hand, cutting him off as he's done to Mother for as long as I can remember. "Not to worry, Father. Happy to help."

Des meets my eyes and nods his gratitude that I didn't forget the task he asked me to complete. He wanted me to look into the discrepancy, and I found quite the gaping hole in our books. Before the day is done, it will be rectified.

Father waves his hand to dismiss the topic. "We can discuss the tariffs later. I wish to raise them, and that would make us even in what we owe Drexdenberg."

"Raise the tariffs?" Des repeats, his eyes narrowing.

"Did you really think the price would never go up?"

Des' gaze fixes on Father, and I know it won't be as simple as all that. "King Ronin and I look forward to discussing this with you. But as we haven't signed anything to agree on a raise in the tariff, you'll give us what you owe."

Father changes the subject in lieu of actually admitting to any wrongdoing. He rubs his temples as if Lily's whole situation is beyond his understanding. "Why? Why would Klein do something like that? Why would he fake your death?"

Lily is silent, though I'm not sure any of us actually expect she'll answer for a madman's crimes.

My voice comes out low through my teeth, my fists clenched. "I want the General's job and title revoked. I want a public apology, and then I want his head for trying to murder my future wife."

Just like that, Father's face irons of all its fear. He's the ruler now, not a dad. To be fair, he's never really been all that dad-like, so it's not too hard a transition. "I will deal with the General. Until then, the girl is to be kept in the palace. We need to work on our story before misinformation gets out."

My nose crinkles. "Our story? We know the story. I just told you the story."

"The betrayal I feel right now would be chaos in the hearts of our people. They'll be told..." I can see Father carefully crafting a web of stories he's growing more convinced of by the second. And just like that, his face looks unaffected, his tone conversational. "Lilya Klein ran away when she saw her classmates murdered. The General presumed her among the dead, because her name was listed on the classroom roster. He's been a broken man for years, but now he's whole again since his young flower has returned. Lily, you had some sort of insanity fit and ran away to Neutral Territory, where you've been processing the deaths of your classmates ever since. Alexavier found you not too long ago, and it was love at second sight."

Mother picks up her martini and drinks it down to the olive, swallowing any protest about how awful this whole thing is.

Father praises his own idea when it becomes clear no one else is going to. "Oo, I like that. Love at second sight. I'll set the court minstrel to compose a song with that title. It can be played at the wedding." Then his mouth pulls in distaste. "And Alexavier didn't *find* Lilya," he corrects himself. He's the only one who can get away with that particular crime. "That's so droll. He *rescued* her." Father tilts his head back, grinning. "Yes, that's much better. Alexavier rescued her from a shifter's attack, which is how she got that hideous scar, but he loved her anyway, even though she's deformed. Then the two of them fell in love—childhood playmates, together again." His eyes fix on me, as if he can't see the steam rolling off of me at the many offenses laced through his fictional account. "You're to be married in the spring. We'll expect an heir in a year's time, and then the fae throne is secure. Everyone can rejoice."

I struggle with the bile that rises, and though I've seen him do this sort of thing before, it's the first time I'm truly sickened by it all.

8

THE STORIES WE TELL

ALEXAVIER

A woebegone bleat escapes Lily's lips, tearing at my heart that this is how her meeting my parents is going.

If looks could kill, my parents would be torn through by the temper in Salem's glare. "If ye ever wonder why my people don't trust the fae, this is why. Putting all the blame on a shifter for crimes your General set in motion. Making the lass who was almost murdered lie to cover for the murderer."

Father motions to Lily. "Forgive me, but is that or is that not the work of a shifter who disfigured the future queen of Faveda? The only thing fudged is the timeline."

I'm going to rule Faveda one day, and I'm not willing to wait this out, playing along with a lie that was never mine. "The point in telling you the truth was so that lies wouldn't have space to fester. I said I want the General gone, and that's what's going to happen. As future king, I have every right to protect my bride from the man who tried to murder her. I have no use for anyone on my cabinet who has such deadly skeletons in his closet."

Mother pauses drowning her true opinions in her second or third martini to shoot me a dubious look, as if to say "good luck finding someone innocent on the cabinet."

Father huffs. "What do you propose, then?"

"Prison, at the very least," I rule. My body feels like it's lengthening, like I'm somehow taller and ready to take the reins on something as big as this. "A man dropped his own daughter off in shifter territory and abandoned her. A lifetime rotting in our cells will be sufficient if a beheading is off the table."

Father straightens the curtains so Des is safe from the sunlight. "You know we don't condone capital punishment of our own kind."

My father is not in charge in this moment. He's lost his chance to do the right thing for his people. For his family. I make that clear when I deliver the plan without leaving room for argument. "The General is not 'our kind' if this is what he does to his own. But fine. Prison. No hearing. The absolute truth to the public. I don't care if they feel unsafe about it all. They should. They've been lied to every time that man opened his mouth and claimed to care about them."

I run my hand through my hair, taking in Lily's closed mouth and the ashen look on her face when Des leads her to the chaise lounge and sits her down. She's utterly destroyed, and my stomach twists at the sight of it.

My voice is steady, though I want nothing more than to take her away from here. "We'll be married when Lily deems she's ready, and if you don't bother her with more lies and nonsense, you might just be invited." I can't tear my eyes away from her devastation, so I swallow hard and drink in the sight of it, locking the image in my heart to torment myself with it whenever I like. "And we'll have children whenever she feels it's time. There will be no more discussion about it. I look forward to seeing how you'll apologize to her tomorrow."

Father's long pause tricks me into thinking I have a voice, a choice. I normally don't put my foot down on anything because, well, it's not my throne yet. But it will be, and I'm tired of watching the mess pile up.

When Father rolls back his shoulders, I see defiance setting in deep. His voice comes out to the tune of a command, and though I don't hold much affection for the man, I've never outright hated him as much as I do in this moment. "How it's going to go is that the General and I will have words about what happened so many years ago. He will be reprimanded in private, not in public. The people have no need to fear their leaders, and that's all this would do. Lilya, you are whole and well, are you not?"

She gazes up at him through watery eyes, her chin firmly set. "No, I am not whole. No, I am not well."

"Then you have no business marrying a prince," he rules, taking the breath from my lungs and holding it in his tight fist. "I'll ask again. Lilya Klein, you are whole and well, are you not?"

Her tears still, her once trembling body locks down in a complete freeze that makes her look ready to pounce. "I am whole and well enough to marry Lexi. I am whole and well enough to listen and care about the people of Faveda —a skill that after all these years, you still have never learned."

Good. Don't let him knock you down. It's moments like these where I can see she's my equal, that she'll play the game, but she won't be completely played.

Father holds her gaze a few beats and then shakes off the tension with a smile I cannot imagine how he produces. He slaps his hands together, as if we're talking about something exciting. I hate it when he shifts personalities so suddenly like this. I've always found if off-putting, but Lily looks horrified. "We'll have a grand announcement later this week. After a public reunion between the General and his lost daughter who's been found, we'll announce to the nation that my son has finally found his bride. They need some good news. The Gorgonell chewed a hole in the iron fence."

My eyes widen. "Did he escape?"

"No, and the hole has been repaired. The beast is still trapped in the Stone Graveyard, but it could have been a disaster. People are talking about how devastating it could've been."

My jaw sets in a firm line. "That's a relief. But Father, I don't want Lily near the General."

Father's glare sneaks back in, polluting his feigned cheeriness. "Lilya's announcement will happen in the order

I've expressed, or the marriage doesn't happen at all. Come, Kloe. There's much to prepare. The people will no doubt be celebrating all night. Goodness knows, the territory needs this." He holds his arm out to Mother in what looks like an invitation, but I understand, as does she, that it's really a command the moment he snaps his fingers at her. Mother wobbles on her heels as she follows where he demands.

I vow to never control Lily like that.

They exit, and the four of us gape at each other in various degrees of shock and worry. Des opens his mouth, but Salem holds up his hand. "Not until we're in the room. They have their plan, and we'll have ours."

I move to offer my arm to Lily, but Des beats me to it. He sticks tight to her left, with Salem stealing the other side. The four of us make our way back to my room, where I can finally exhale. Des is wholly focused on Lily, giving no one else the opportunity to comfort her. "Sit down, blue eyes. Salem, can you get her some water?"

"It'll be okay, Lily-girl," I offer.

She takes two steps toward me, and I realize how much I've missed her touch. I reach for her, but freeze when her tremulous eyes narrow into a vengeful glare that lands in my direction.

"How could you do that to me?" Her shout is shaky but no less venomous. It shocks me to my core when her hand pulls back, and she punches me across the face.

9

HELP VERSUS CONTROL

LILYA

My smile is fake. Can't the soldiers see that? Or have they grown so used to the façade that the real thing looks off to them? I can't decide if I despise them or if I feel bad for them.

Nothing. I nothing them. I can't feel happiness when the soldiers bow to us as we stroll through the barracks toward the exit. I'm told the soldiers are excited that their prince now has the promise of a princess. I almost wish for the boos and the curses flung at me in earnest honesty in Drexenberg. They hated me to my face, but as I stare at the smiles of the men my age who have the calculating look of sizing me up to see what assets I possess that they covet, I wish for the outright hatred. Their eyes rake over my body appraisingly, then tear away from my face when the scars are too hideous to look at directly. I can see their pity. Lexi is the most eligible bachelor in the kingdom, sought after by the finest women (as his father has been so kind as to inform me), yet somehow he ended up with a "deformed" fae.

The worst part is I still can barely stand to look at him.

It's been a full day, and I'm no less livid than I was when Lexi ditched the plan to keep my identity a secret and threw me to the wolves. He's apologized, but I don't want to hear it. I'm in the mess now, deeply set in the muck I'm now expected to navigate flawlessly.

So I play the role of the loving new fiancée I'm supposed to convince the soldiers I am. We're leaving the barracks after telling them the insider information of our engagement, so they know how best to guard us on the big day of the announcement. My stomach is in knots, even though I've been assured the General isn't there. He's in the palace, so I've been shunted off the grounds to greet the troops that Lexi and I will one day command.

The General hasn't been allowed to see me. In fact, we won't see each other until the grand unveiling and engage- ment announcement. I want nothing to do with any of it, any of them. I want to take Des and Salem and run far, far away.

But this is the job. This is what I signed on for. Uniting the three territories isn't going to be easy, but I never dreamed it would be this horrible. I looked up to King Fairbucks as a girl, back when I was too young to know better. He gave me treats. He smiled at me when the General was a monster.

Now I understand that monsters come in all forms. Some even smile.

I spent the morning in lessons, trying to cram in as much knowledge as Lexi's tutors could shove in my head. Then there were the elocution lessons, ironing out my "village idiot-speak" as they so charmingly put it. I'm to talk proper, so I make sure to do a perfect imitation of Lexi's mother in public, so I sound the part. It's an unused muscle, but I can fake decorum well enough, I've learned.

I slept in Des' arms last night, sneaking from Lexi's room to somewhere I felt safe. My hand needs to be on Des' chest at all times these days. With all the deceitfulness swarming around me, I need something true, and Des is my one true thing. I breathe easier when my hand is on his chest. I can think clearer. I crave truth in this world of lies.

Salem hasn't talked much, but he warms my toes while I sleep, so I think maybe that means he's making good on his word to watch over me while I'm living in Faveda. He's stuck to his wolf form since the meeting with Lexi's parents. I haven't seen his handsome face since.

Lexi doesn't sleep with us.

My fiancé's smile fades the moment we climb inside the carriage to return to the palace. He closes his eyes and leans his head back, looking more exhausted than usual. He's got bags under his eyes and actually looks like he's in pain.

I'm angry with him, but he's still my Lexi. Theirs but mine. I want to comfort him and also push him away. It's hard to reconcile those two men, not knowing which I'm sitting beside. I don't trust him, which is something I never thought I'd say.

Lexi runs his hand over his face. "I know you're not ready to speak to me, but we really should discuss when the wedding should happen. If you want a say, I'd like to hear your opinion. My father is controlling too much; we need to be firm on something."

My choice to keep quiet feels like it's come to an end, so I choose my words carefully, since they're the first I've spoken directly to him in far too long. "The sooner the better. Get it over with. Next week. Next month. I don't care about the particulars."

He leans his elbow on the carriage wall, his knuckle between his teeth while he chews on his response before it tumbles out unchecked. "I suppose apologizing again wouldn't help matters."

"No. I don't need to hear it. You made a choice. It is what it is. I can be civil, but I don't trust you. Luckily, I don't know of a single fae marriage that's built on trust, so we should fit right in."

"I told them the truth. That's my biggest crime, I hope you realize."

I can't believe this is the path he's taking. I scoff at him. "Your crime is that you thought you knew best, so you went over my head and changed the plan without telling me a single thing. We agreed we wouldn't tell them about my childhood. Then you waltzed in there and told them the most painful part of my past in the first minute they re-met me, as if that's all I am." I iron out a crease in my white silk dress. Kloe Fairbucks always notices the wrinkles. She's not mean about it, but I know she sees them. "Well,

I've got news for you: I barely think about the General and all of it. I barely remember a lick of it," I lie. "We had a plan, and you went rogue. We were supposed to be a team."

Lexi doesn't argue, though I can tell by his raised shoulders that he wants to. "You're right. Even if I stand by telling them what I did, I should've talked to you about it. I thought I knew better."

"About me. You thought you knew me better than me. Your father speaks for your mom, I hope you realize. He doesn't give her a voice in her own home. That's what you did to me."

He hangs his head, and I see clearly his self-loathing. "I was wrong. We were supposed to be a team, the four of us. I can't take it all back. I can only promise not to do that in the future."

I push at my gown again. It's so thin, it's nearly transparent, especially in the sunlight. But I can see the creases, mocking me as I try to control them. I'm not wearing a bra or underwear, since every line can be seen through the thin fabric. I'm not sure how the seamstress talked me into that, but I regretted it the second I left the palace this morning. It's nearly time for the announcement, and I want desperately to hide out inside.

Lexi unleashes a heavy sigh. "I did something you're not going to like. In my defense, I'm an idiot."

"That's your defense?"

"I suppose begging for your pity has a better likelihood of success than pleading for forgiveness."

It's the first time I've almost smiled for real in a while.

"Okay. What am I supposed to shake my head at you for doing?"

He slides a note from his pocket, handing it to me without looking in my direction. "It's from the General, sent to you. It arrived this morning, sealed with his signet ring."

My blood goes cold as I freeze. "If he sealed it, why is the envelope open?"

"I opened it. I was being controlling again, apparently. I guess I have a problem with that. I wanted to know what he would say to his daughter after all these years. I wanted to know what a vile man he truly is. I wanted… My intention was to destroy the letter so you never had to look at it, but I realize now that's just another version of making a decision without your input. Apparently that's bad. I admit, I'm new to the whole marriage thing myself."

I scowl at him. "You have a problem. I can't believe you did that. Did you know this is my very first piece of mail? They don't deliver post in Neutral Territory. My very first piece of mail in my life, and you opened it." I turn in my seat to face him, which perks him up through his penitent expression. He straightens, as if I'm readying to forgive him for everything, including this latest crime. "Lexi, you are a very stupid boy if you think that I'm going to marry you and let you decide every little thing. You are not in charge of what mail I get or who I tell my story to. You are in charge of being a good man, and that is all. Good men don't take control that doesn't belong to them."

He nods. "I'm going to be in charge of a kingdom, Lily.

I'll make decisions for other people all day every day. So will you. I'm new at this, and very bad at it." He takes a chance and places his hand on mine.

"I'm not your subject. I'm…" I want to tell him I'm his wife, but I've never seen fae men value their women's voices all that much. I want to be more to him than someone concerned with only appearances. "I'm your Lily-girl. Your partner."

His eyes close, looking pained at the use of my nickname. "You're right."

"So instead of controlling me, focus on the things around you that need changing, so I don't need this much protection. And I've got news for you; I've been handling my past by myself this entire time without you, and I came out the other end just fine."

"You certainly did. And I had nothing to do with that. It was all you. My help sometimes isn't all that helpful."

I push him one further. "Your 'help' is sometimes another word for 'control,' and it stops today."

He nods, and something about the firmness in his jaw makes me believe he really is sorry, and he really will try to get better at this. "Today," he vows.

I touch his cheek because I've missed him so very much. I've wanted to be near him, even when I've wanted to push him away. He's going to try, and I'm going to be patient while he learns how to have a partner in this.

Lexi kisses my fingertips, and I realize how much more I want from him. It's been too long since I've tasted his tongue, too long since I've felt myself relax in his arms. "I'm still mad," I admit.

"In your defense, I was very, very stupid. Twice, now."

My eyes glint at the letter in my other hand. "My father wrote me a letter."

"He did."

I close my eyes. "I'm not sure I want to read it."

Lexi stiffens but doesn't release my hand. "I suppose that's your prerogative. I can respect your decision."

The corner of my mouth twitches. "Good answer. You passed the test. Maybe you're not so stupid after all."

He grins, as if I've just told him he's handsome. "Let me take you to the waterfalls tomorrow. The ones we used to collect pinecones near. Just us. I haven't been with you in so long."

"You're with me now. You've been by my side all day!"

"You know what I mean. I just got you back where you'll actually look at me. I want more of this."

"Okay." I stretch the fabric again with a huff of frustration. "I can't wear this for the announcement. I have to change. The seamstress is going to be upset about all the creases in my dress. She counts them, you know."

"She does not. A fae seamstress would never be so very vain."

It's a well-timed joke, and draws out my smile.

"You should congratulate me for being such a gentleman all day. I can see clear through your slip of a dress, as can every other man in the territory, yet I haven't made an unsavory pass at you, and haven't murdered the men who've stared at your nipples while you waved."

My cheeks heat up. "The seamstress promised it wasn't see-through."

"A fae who lies? Well, I never. The scandal of it all." He chuckles, finally relaxing in his seat. "She designed it that way on purpose to make sure every man can see how lucky I am, and every woman knows how beautiful you are, so they don't fool themselves into thinking they have a chance with me. It's really a compliment, wrapped in a lie. Don't be too hard on Dulcinea. She means well."

His arm finds its way around me, and though the trust between us isn't quite there for all the things it should be, I decide to give up on my frustrations for the moment and relax into his side. "When are we going to tell your parents and the territory that I'm already married to Des?"

"I suppose that's the sort of thing the four of us should agree on, and I shouldn't go off-book."

I gasp. "He can be taught!"

Lexi chuckles, kissing my naked shoulder. "I know you sneaked into Des' room last night."

I tuck a loose curl behind my ear. "I couldn't sleep."

"With me. You couldn't sleep with me."

I shrug, not willing to apologize for it. "I was back in your room before anyone else woke. No one saw me."

Lexi sighs. "Luckily, the notion of a vampire and a fae hooking up is about as foreign to everyone as an elephant mating with a mosquito, so they don't suspect anything.

Still, I think it's best we all make a plan about this, since we're on speaking terms now."

"Stop saying the right thing just so I'll kiss you. It's not going to work."

His lips travel to the thin strap of my dress, and I can feel him grinning against my skin. "Pity. What do you say about this scrap of fabric here? It's barely creased at all. One might assume we're not on the verge of marriage with how unruffled you look." His hand runs down my side just as the carriage comes to a halt.

I lift my chin. "Let's not get ahead of ourselves. I've only just barely forgiven you."

Then Lexi does something so startling, I can feel my blush creeping clear down my entire body. He takes my strap in his teeth and drags it down my shoulder.

"Wicked prince," I scold him quietly.

He kisses my bare skin, sending heat and shivers through me simultaneously. "You wouldn't have me any other way."

He slides it right back into place as quickly as it fell when the carriage door opens. Lexi's dark chuckle tells me he's very much through with sleeping alone.

I expect the driver to be the one who greets us in the twilight, but the smile that welcomes me when I step out of the carriage is the dazzling grin of King Ronin—Des' great-grandfather, and one of my few friends in the world. "Hello, darling. Did you miss me?"

10

FAE ON THE FLOOR

DESTINO

King Ronin's never spoken to me this much in the span of an entire month, yet when Lily's around, he's simply popping with conversation. He comes to life around her. It doesn't help that the fae are complete perverts, and the seamstress dressed my wife yet again in a completely sheer white dress that's silkier than anything I've ever touched. I don't like that she's so relaxed around Great-grandfather, that he makes her laugh, that he's always the first to offer her his arm. It's the first time outside our bedroom that she's been calm enough to smile naturally, instead of accessing that awful false grin she wears for Alex's parents.

It's not jealousy, because there's no flirt in her voice for King Ronin. I don't know what it is, but it rubs me the wrong way.

Alex is glued to her other side, as he should be. This is

his hometown, and she's going to marry him. Next month. She's going to marry him next month. Our plan is actually going to happen. The territories are one step closer to uniting, whether they know it's coming or not. Whether they like it or not.

"Dinner is served, your majesties," one of the servants announces to us, drawing us from the receiving room into the dining room.

I sit beside King Ronin, because that's what's expected. Keep the vampires and shifters on one side of the table to make sure no one gets too close for the delicate fae's comfort. I do my best not to steal glances at Lily's breasts, but honestly, they're so beautifully displayed through the thin material, my fingers ache to stroke the taut peaks. She slept coiled around me in nothing but my shirt and a lacy scrap of underwear last night, and I loved it. She said she wanted to sleep in my shirt because she wanted to smell like me. Said just my scent made her feel safe. If there are other things that make a man feel like he can lift a house off the ground, I don't know if any are better than a shy compliment like that.

Salem looks around, and it's then I realize we're one seat short. It's the first time he's been a man in days, and I'll admit, it's nice to be able to talk to my best friend.

Alex stands. "Sorry, Salem. I'll go get you a chair, brother."

King Fairbucks snaps his fingers and points to the floor where the missing chair should be. "Don't trouble yourself. The shifter can eat off the floor, as he no doubt prefers."

Alex hisses his disapproval, and I keep my mouth shut, as I'm supposed to do. We all handle our own parents. That's the deal.

Lily's unaware of the deal, apparently, because her expression goes cold as she fixes the king with a stony glare. "He's a man, not a dog. Here, Salem. Take my chair."

Then before anyone can stop her, she marches around the table and plops down on the floor near the end of the table on Ronin's other side. The "lesser than fae" side. The fine material isn't made for sitting on floors, but Lily ignores that, as well as Queen Kloe's shriek of disapproval. "There's no need for you to sit on the floor!"

"Why?" Lily protests. "Is there something demeaning about a person eating off the floor? Is that what we do to each other in this house? To fellow royalty?"

King Fairbucks has the gall to roll his eyes. "Do save your youthful ideals for someone with more patience than I have. King Ronin, have you ever heard such foolishness?"

The look he shoots my great-grandfather is filled with a warning. King Ronin doesn't like shifters any more than the next fae or vamp, but he's not as disrespectful as the fae can be. It's a testament to how much power Lily truly does hold when Great-grandfather doesn't brush her off with an aloof comment, but instead nods thoughtfully. "Lily makes a valid point. I think our ways of doing things might be outdated, and in need of thorough reconsideration. Actual-ly," he says as he stands. "Here, Prince Salem. Have my seat, Son."

Son. It's a thing he's started calling Alex and me, and

now Salem. I like it, I think, but it's such a stark contrast from having to call my great-grandfather by his proper title most of his life. It's only when Lily came around that anyone's ever dared drop the "king" when addressing him. I'm not quite there yet.

Alex and I also stand, offering him our chairs.

Salem's head snaps in King Ronin's direction. I'm not sure if he's more shocked that the king is offering him his seat, or if being called "son" for the first time in over a decade by anyone throws him more. He doesn't do well with a spotlight, so instead he trots around to Lily's side and drops down. "What did I tell ye about never being on your knees again?"

"You matter," Lily says with such ferocity through clenched teeth that my insides shake. "I can go along with everything else, but this is disgusting. I won't laugh at a joke made at your expense. I can't play nice about some-thing this cruel. I don't care how much you hate me."

Salem's eyebrows shoot toward his hairline. "What? I don't hate ye."

She rolls her eyes. "Fine. The fact that you don't like me near you doesn't change me. *I* change me, not stupid social rules, not old prejudices. Me. And I've decided not to be a ruler who sits above her peers, so don't try to take this away from me."

It's clear to me where she's coming from, though Salem looks like he has no clue. He avoids touching her, being too close, because I know he's one bat of an eyelash away from devouring her whole, so incredible is his love for her. How I wish they would stop being so skittish and let themselves relax around each other.

Salem's voice has a gentle note to its gruff nature. "S'alright, Lily. It doesn't bother me. This is just how the fae are."

"*I'm* fae," she protests as he stands, lifting her off the floor in a fluid motion. "I live here now, right?" She looks around to meet Alex's eyes to confirm.

Alex nods. "Of course you do. This is your home, Lily-girl."

Her eyes sweep from Queen Kloe to King Fairbucks. "Then in my home, I'd like my friends treated with respect. I can't imagine such well-bred fae as yourselves would take issue with that." It's a compliment wrapped in a threat. If there's ever any doubt she's fae, that seals it. It's impossible to watch her stand up to monarchs and be unimpressed.

King Fairbucks dons a simpering smile. "Of course we can be civil. What do you take us for, mongrels? And I know that you'll be just as magnanimous when the General comes to dinners, smiling and sitting beside him and whatnot."

King Ronin stiffens beside me, and it's then I realize no one has caught him up on the details—large or invisibly small. "Do refresh my memory. Is there a problem Lily's having with General Klein? She's only been here a week. Surely there haven't been any unpleasantries already."

King Fairbucks flicks his wrist. "It's a sad tale. General

Klein had a daughter years ago, as you know, who we assumed died from the vampire attack in her classroom when she was eight years old. Only the girl merely appeared dead, and was listed among the deceased by mistake. She underwent a shock of some sort—you know how delicate females can be—and wandered into Jacoba, where she was attacked by a shifter." I'm sick to my stomach when King Fairbucks motions to his cheek. "That's how she became disfigured. She was so traumatized by watching her classmates come to ruin that she completely forgot who she was and wandered into Neutral Territory, where she's been living ever since. My Alexavier rescued her, and discovered she was none other than Lilya Klein—his childhood friend. He was quite taken with her, despite her deformity."

I cringe at his words, my fists clenched at my sides.

Queen Kloe gestures with her martini in her hand, spilling a few drops on the white tablecloth. "And there you have it. Our son is engaged to be married next month. We couldn't be happier to have Lilya as our daughter. Long live the Fairbucks rule."

"Quiet, Kloe," King Fairbucks chides in a snap of coldness that spreads an awkward silence through the room.

King Ronin's tongue slowly sweeps over his top row of teeth when he takes in Lily's deadened eyes and gaunt complexion. He may not understand which parts of the story are a deception, but he reads her well enough to spot a drowning woman, suffocating under the weight of a fae-spun lie.

It's all I can do to keep myself under control, and I've known about the stupid lie we're going to have to help sell for a few days now. I watch the deception crash over King Ronin. He doesn't allow it to mess with his posture or composure. It's… It's remarkable, actually. I need to learn that skill. I'm three breaths away from choking King Fairbucks out in front of his family.

When Great-grandfather finally speaks, his voice is composed. "My, what a happy ending. Your father must be so pleased you're back. What's the General's reaction been to the news? If it was my child I'd been parted from, I can't imagine letting her out of my sight for a moment."

King Fairbucks bats his hand with a relaxed smile. "Oh, General Klein is overjoyed. Anxious to see her."

"He is?" King Ronin lets out a light laugh meant for needling. He plays the game of the fae well. "He can't be too anxious to be with his daughter if he's not here. How unruly is your land if the General can't have an evening off to spend with his long-lost daughter?"

King Fairbucks' eyes narrow, though his smile doesn't fade. "They haven't actually been reunited yet. We're saving that for the festival tomorrow night. I suppose since you've come by, you should tag along so you can see the grand reunion firsthand. We'll have them greet each other for the first time on the stage, and then Alexavier will announce his engagement to Lilya. It'll be splendid."

King Ronin's eyes flick to Lily. "I see. How overjoyed you must be."

"Overjoyed," she echoes, deadpanned. She says the right

words, but she doesn't hold back her true terror from King Ronin, which shines in her eyes when she looks up at him. No doubt he sees that she has no qualms murdering attackers with a silver dagger, but the mere prospect of a conversation with her father has her checking the exits.

Salem angles his body so his shoulder is bracing her from behind—support and strength should she need it. I move toward them, standing on her other side so she knows we're in this together. No one can see my hand except Salem, so I run my knuckle down her spine to remind her that if the General wants to get at her again, he'll have to go through us.

King Ronin touches his lips as he takes in the tenor of the room. "Everyone will take a seat now. I've no need for one." He motions for Salem to take his spot, and we all obey. Great-grandfather has that way about him. He has little patience for fae games. "I'll be in the receiving room. Alexavier, I have a gift for you and your future bride I'd be delighted to give you after you finish dining. I was going to wait until later, but you really should have it before the big festival. A token of generosity from the vampires to the fae on this joyous occasion. Do stop by when you're done. Excuse me."

There's a hint just subtle enough for us to catch that old King Ronin's hatching a plan.

"That is your future daughter-in-law, I hope you know," Alex says in a low voice the moment King Ronin leaves. He points at Lily, whom all this controversy has been about, but she hasn't said much about it all. Perhaps she's learning that having a voice doesn't actually mean getting to use it. Alex motions to us. "And those are my best friends. Since everything about you is faked, I should think you'd be able to spot the real thing when it's staring you in the face. Your ways of ruling are small-minded. My rule will not be small. My wife will not feel unsafe in her own home. My brother will not eat off the floor." He moves to stand in front of us, his arm reaching around behind him to grip Lily's hip. She leans into his spine and closes her eyes.

It's sweet, Lily learning to lean while Alex learns to stand without trampling the people he loves. I guess we're all growing up.

Alex's voice is dripping with contempt. "The General is not to go near Lily—before or after the public announcement. You can have your sweeping, tear-filled displays because she's agreed to it, but he will not come into this palace under any circumstances. If I have to wait until the crown is on my head to see his head removed, so be it." When King Fairbucks opens his mouth to protest, Alex raises his hand to shut his father up. I'm astonished at the poetry of the king being shut up, when it's usually him bulldozing others. "If General Klein tries to murder her again after the announcement of our engagement is made, it will be clear you have a problem in your cabinet. It will make you look weak, like you cannot control the snakes you pretend to command."

King Fairbucks swallows a sip of his wine and takes his

time setting down his glass. "Very well. I'll continue to keep him off the palace grounds even after the announcement."

Then, without a discussion or nod of a head, the four of us exit, moving as one away from the meal that's turned all of our stomachs. I lead us down the hallways toward the receiving room, hoping King Ronin has a plan.

11

MAKING HISTORY AND BREAKING THE FUTURE

LILYA

The second Salem locks the door to the receiving room behind us, my façade of self-control crumbles. I throw my arms around Lexi, holding him through his fury at watching his parents behave so horribly. "It will not be that way when you rule. You are kind and good. You respect your people, so you won't lie to them when it's your turn to decide what they hear."

"When *we* rule, you mean," Lexi corrects me. "That you still believe in our people after hearing that? I'm amazed by you. We'll figure this out. So long as you don't run away, we'll make the territory better. All three territories."

I nod eagerly, then lift up on my toes to peck his lips. "You will be a noble king someday."

"Instead of a wicked prince?" At my wry smirk, his shoulders lower. "I will never force you to be a silent queen," Lexi promises, and then steps back to shake out his nerves, cracking his knuckles a few times and managing an anxious smile.

I turn to Des, who kisses my lips in a quick promise that somehow, someway, life won't always feel like this. I touch his heart and breathe, finally feeling my ribs expand to their full potential as his heart convinces me that there is truth still left in the world.

I step away and meet Salem's eyes, taking in his nod as he stands off to the side near the door. He's protecting us, standing guard just in case. That's how he loves, and I'm lucky to be counted among the few he cares about, however strangely.

When I turn to Ronin, he's composed with his spine straight, looking like a king plopped smack in the middle of a chaos he didn't create but must now maneuver. He's on the outside of our group perhaps because that's where he feels he belongs.

I decide I'm not okay with that, so my feet scamper in his direction and my arms throw themselves around his neck. His eyes close as our hug lifts me off my toes, the way all good hugs should. His cheek is smooth as his lips find my ear. "How I've needed to see your face, my darling."

"I missed you terribly. You really came all this way just to see us?"

"I promised to go with you every step of the way through this thing, and I intend to make good on my word. I'm your family, aren't I? We're supposed to do things like that for each other?"

I'm so overwhelmed with love for this man that I kiss

his cheek, drawing out a chuckle and a blush from him as he slides me down his body so I'm standing before him. Ronin waves his hand to Des. "Son, I see you haven't torn the heads off any corrupt monarchs. Well done. Though, I admit, I was tempted just now. I look forward to hearing the actual reason General Klein is too busy to be reunited with his daughter." His eyes burn into mine. "I recall a troubling slip of a conversation where you told me that what you were most scared of was your father. I trust nothing has changed in that department?"

I swallow hard. "I haven't seen him yet."

He shakes his head. "Lilya Klein, daughter of General Klein. I daresay I probably saw you scampering around the palace when you were young, when I was here visiting to discuss affairs with General Klein and King Fairbucks." He thumbs the bottom of the scar on my cheek. "I can't believe he's capable of something so horrible. And yet, perhaps I can."

Des comes over to us but stops two feet away. Ronin reaches out and grabs him by the shoulder, pulling him in so one arm is wrapped around me, and the other is around Des.

Des stiffens, his eyes wide. I know he's used to hugging the guys, but it breaks my heart a little that this looks like it might be the first time he's been hugged by Ronin in his adult life. "Um, are you feeling well, King Ronin?"

"I think it's time you boys stopped using my title. You're my great-grandson, after all. And we're in this together."

Des shoots me a look of worry. "What have you done,

blue eyes? Have you broken the King of Drexdenberg? Have you used your fae trickery on him to get him to be kind?" His hand feels Ronin's forehead to check for a fever. "Perhaps you've taken ill."

Ronin laughs through his nose and releases Des but holds me firmly to his side. "Actually, I've been feeling more clear-headed than ever this week. Maybe it's the last of the poison leaving my system. Maybe it's that I'm excited for the first time ever that Drexdenberg will fall to good and capable hands. I don't feel the crushing weight of doing it alone anymore. I have my son." He smiles at Des, who looks so shocked, I almost feel bad for him. Then he gazes down at me, a smile of pure indulgence touching his eyes as he drinks in my features. "And I have my girl. The future looks bright, indeed." His head lifts to address us all as he brings me to sit beside him on the white chaise lounge. "Now, I'd like the true version of the story, if you please."

It's the one time I wish Lexi would take over, and the one time he grows up and doesn't, leaving the telling of my story to me. I cover the basics the guys already know, leaving the more damning details to myself.

Classmates died in a freak accident (I don't fill him in on the details of that). General Klein wanted to get rid of me. Shifter tearing up my face. Escape to Neutral Territory at eight years old.

Ronin's jaw ticks at each detail, but he soaks in the entirety of it, and finally speaks when I'm finished. "That version is quite different than the one King Fairbucks spun in the dining room. I trust he knows the truth but is going in a different direction?"

I nod, and Ronin doesn't skate over my pain. He cups my cheek, giving me a shred of sweetness to support me through this grim situation. I like that he's not afraid to touch my scar. After being referred to as "deformed," it's redemptive to be caressed in my ugly spots. "I don't want to see my father," I admit in a whisper.

Ronin nods solemnly. "It looks like the cheery story that will be spun to the public about General Klein is out of our hands, I'm afraid. I've known King Fairbucks a great many years, so giving him this one might be inevitable. But what I can offer you is me—a poor pittance, I'm sure. Would it help if I promised to stay here by your side through it all, so there's no chance General Klein will be able to harm you again?"

I sink into his embrace, relieved he isn't willing to abandon me when I'm this aware of how badly everything could go wrong. "Thank you."

"Of course." His arm stays around me as he continues. "Now, to all my future rulers, let me impart this wisdom: when we give in on one point, we must look for where we can take back another advantage for ourselves. We give King Fairbucks and General Klein the rose-painted reunion they desire, and we take the wedding."

My nose scrunches. "We've always had the wedding, though. It's next month."

"Ah, but what you don't know is that the apple rosé hasn't been ordered."

I don't have any clue what that means, but Lexi's nostrils flare. "But apple rosé takes two months to cure. Father assured me he ordered it the first day he learned of our engagement."

Ronin nods once. "Exactly. The traditional wine is always served at royal fae weddings. I checked with the kitchen staff, and it hasn't been ordered. It isn't being made at all."

"They don't think we'll go through with the wedding," Lexi concludes, his tone grim. "Well, they're wrong. We love each other."

I rally every time I'm reminded of how sure Lexi is of us.

Ronin holds up his finger. "Ah, but it's not your love they doubt. Love had nothing to do with your parents' marriage, Alexavier. It's a daughter with a past they don't want that's driving this. A girl they can't trick into being quiet. They have no intention of letting you go through with this wedding. I don't know their plan, but it is most certainly not to let the two of you wed."

My lips press in a firm line. "That's such a small detail, though. Are we really making this big a stink about wine?"

Lexi casts me a pained look. "Have you read the letter sent from the General to you yet?"

My eyes narrow at him. "No, but you have. Why don't you share with the room what my mail says?"

Lexi lowers his chin. "It's a threat to keep your mouth shut. That you know why he tried to put you down quietly, and if you cause a problem, he'll shed light on the real reason he tried to kill you."

The room goes quiet, and though I haven't eaten a thing, I'm worried I might vomit.

Ronin looks down at my fear, not with that beam that shines for me, but with a question mark I wish wasn't there. "What reason is that?"

I stand, moving out of Ronin's reach, hugging myself around the middle. "No reason that matters right now."

Des' hand finds my back. "You're looking for logic in a murderer's musings? He tried to kill his own child. I don't care what insipid reason he concocts. It's madness. Lily doesn't need to answer for her father's crimes."

I love Des, and I also fear the day he finds out all I've done.

But that day is not today. Today his hand rests on my back because that's where it belongs.

Ronin slaps his hands together, retrieving our scattered focus. "We're giving the fae their father/daughter reunion, but I have something in mind that we can take for ourselves. We cannot let King Fairbucks control this part of the journey, or the course of history will never change. I have marriage documents in my bag that I brought just in case. I can marry the two of you right here, right now. Then there's nothing they can do about it."

My heart goes still and all breath leaves me. "You mean... Married today? Right now? But we haven't even made the public engagement announcement!"

"You can surprise your in-laws by making it a marriage

announcement. Take control of this throne, or King Fair-bucks will choke all that's good in you until the day you die. You've been here barely a week, and it's already start-ed." Ronin's warning comes at me in earnest, and I see the sincerity in his eyes.

My gaze cuts to Lexi, who's burning with the same passion to move this leg of the plan forward this very minute. "I have the wedding rings upstairs." He waits for my nod, which I manage as all the moisture leaves my throat. Then Lexi turns to the door, his hand stilling on the knob. "This will be an act of war," he tells Ronin. "You understand that, don't you? It's your name on the license as the officiant."

Ronin grins like a wicked cat who's on the brink of trapping a canary. "Funny, I thought marriages were supposed to be an act of love."

Lexi chuckles and then disappears, his feet running until they fade from my hearing.

Ronin turns to Des and me. "I think the evening should go like this: give the fae their tearful father/daughter reunion. Then surprise everyone with a marriage announcement. Then perhaps I'll take a moment to give my blessing, since you were my daughter-in-law first. Best drop all the bombs at once."

Des rubs the nape of his neck. "I guess we're really in it now."

Salem's been quiet through the whole thing, but finally he speaks. "I'll have a carriage ready and waiting behind the palace. I'll make sure it's not one marked as belonging to the palace, but just looks like a normal transport. We can flee to Jacoba if things get out of hand."

"Can you guarantee her safety?" Ronin asks.

Salem shrugs, which isn't very reassuring. "Do ye have a better plan?"

Ronin sighs. "Your borders are closer than mine. I suppose it'll have to do." He pulls out the marriage license and sets it on the table, filling out our names and the date and such.

I'm getting married. Lexi and I are getting married.

When my fiancé trots back into the room, he's confident. His shoulders are rolled back with anticipation beaming from every pore, telling us all that this is what he wants.

I am what he wants. A new world. A new future. With me.

I reach out for Lexi, and he takes my hand. So many flickers of this exact moment play in my mind, my hand much smaller as he pulls me up into tree limbs, over fences and through fields. We'd come back dirty and tired but so very happy. We were children then, but now we're making so many grown-up decisions.

My knees are shaking as I stand in front of Ronin with the guys standing behind us. A respectful quiet brushes over us all as we set to make history, and break the future.

12

TOWARD THE LIGHT

ALEXAVIER

It's loud. I brace myself for it every time, but whenever there's a huge nationwide festival or some big announcement, the charm used to make Father's voice boom out makes the nearest thousand or so wince at the volume. I hold my posture and my smile like the well-bred prince I am, but it's an effort. Flinching is not tolerated when you're the king's son.

The stage is long, a set-up/tear-down contraption that is assembled in front of the palace on days like this, framing us with ivorum that glistens out across the land. We're raised ten feet off the ground so everyone can see us, and there's a line of soldiers to keep the people from clambering too near. We're above them but one of them. It's a powerful picture, and I'm grateful to be part of it today.

Lily is off-stage, hidden behind a partition off to the right and below us, but still separate from the throngs of citizens. She's standing with Ronin, Des and Salem, waiting for her cue. She's changed into a pure white gown that flows to the floor, showing off her trim waist and luminous, subtle curves. The material's not transparent this time, thank goodness. Her hair's been done up, her lavender curls pinned to look like they're spilling out the back of her head. I'm so used to seeing her doused in blood, or sleeping on the cave floor. Today she looks like a fae princess.

She looks like she belongs with me.

Father drones about the bond between he and I, and it's all I can do to fend off my eyeroll. Mother's eyes are glazed over, but she doesn't teeter. No doubt Father's cut short her flow of alcohol until after the big announcement, so she's on her best behavior to earn back her only saving grace. Father brags that he would do anything for his child, as he knows the General would.

General Klein is on the other end of the stage, dressed in his white military jacket and pants. His musculature is still there, though some of the bulk has shifted with age, making him look like a man on the brink of retirement who's held onto his post a few years too long. How I want him off the cabinet. How I long to see him hanged for all he's done.

Lily was… She's… Lily deserved better, and I despise him for taking her away from her home, from me.

Father's voice reaches a crescendo, and he actually manages to sound choked up, so I tune back in to listen to the drivel I'm supposed to be agreeing with.

"So today, I'd like to invite parents to hold tight to their children while you witness this momentous occasion. General Klein thought his daughter lost, but she's been found by your prince, and brought home to us once more. Today he puts down his sword and picks up his heart that's been broken for sixteen long years. My fellow fae, please welcome Lilya Klein as she sees her father for the first time in her adult life!"

I turn toward my true family, watching Des study Lily with anxious eyes as she glides up the steps and onto the stage. Des is gaunt, like he's afraid we're subjecting her to far too much. That this cruelty will push her over the edge.

I'm worried she's going to crumble under the pressure of hundreds of thousands of eyes. I have to remind myself that the girl who was terrified in vampire country knows well the way to play the game in Faveda. Though she's had less training than most, she knows what the people want, so she gives it to them in spades with her chin high and a white silk handkerchief in her hand to dab at invisible tears as she crosses the stage toward her father.

I cannot help my grimace when the two embrace. Fury the likes of which I'm not accustomed to wells up in me, threatening to spill out in a punch aimed at the General's shaking shoulders. The quaking is too overdone to be genuine emotion, but the audience eats it up because that's what they want to see.

Des marches up on the stage, which isn't part of the plan. He's to remain off to the side with Ronin and Salem, only coming up toward the end when we announce our scandal. He can't stomach lies as well as the average fae.

Worry pinches the edges of my grin, and I debate whether or not to pull him back so he doesn't do or say something in front of the entire territory he can't take back. Ronin seems to have the same concerns I do, so when I take a step in Des' direction, Ronin trots onto the stage, a calm expression in place as if this is all part of the schedule of events.

Des takes the attention at center stage from Father and gives a polite bow, addressing the nation with boldness blazing in his eyes. "The nation of Drexdenberg has been more than happy to host the General's daughter while she tried to figure out a way to come home to her loving father." He pauses for the people's awkward applause. They like what's being said, just not the person saying it.

When the day comes that Ronin hands over the crown, Des will be ready. I can tell by the burning determination in his eyes as he presses on. "Seventy-nine shipments of blood that were promised to us by the fae were never delivered until your heroic Prince Alexavier noticed the oversight and immediately rectified the problem. He values us, and we value the fae so much that I personally assured Lilya's safe return home. I have great respect for Prince Alexavier, and when I am King of Drexdenberg in less than a year's time, I look forward to peaceful relations between our territories." He smiles at Father, who keeps his magnanimous smile in place while screaming with his eyes. "King Fairbucks has so graciously informed us that not only will he replace the seventy-nine blood shipments that he lost, but he'll also lower the tariffs, so the people of

Drexdenberg won't have to work so hard to keep from starving. Your king values all life, even the lives that seem perhaps less valuable than your own." Des bows, and I have half a mind to applaud the bastard for his antics, playing the game to the advantage of his kingdom. Father has twisted everything leading up to this, but we're taking control now.

The corners of Des' mouth curve in what can only be viewed as sweet vengeance, from one wicked prince to a corrupt king. "Thank you, King Fairbucks for your generosity. The relations between our kingdom and yours have never been stronger. Perhaps when you come to see us in our castle, you can stay a bit longer next time and really feel the appreciation we have for you."

I fight back a laugh. Father and Mother would never dream of setting foot in Drexdenberg. Most meetings of the monarchs are held in Faveda. Getting the people to picture their stainless, flawless rulers traipsing around with vampires plays to our favor. Maybe they'll be disgusted, but perhaps their minds will start to open, viewing those outside our borders as people, too.

Ronin stands beside Des and bows to Father. "We are most grateful. What a lovely people. What a lovely day. What a lovely girl." He turns to Lily, his eyes meeting hers with... something. I hate that nameless something I can't put my finger on. It bothers me, and by the way she's attached her affections to him, I can tell their friendship will vex me for years to come. "We were delighted to have her in our home."

I do not like him saying things like that to her, but there it is. Lily stands next to the man who was supposed to raise her but tried to kill her, begging with her eyes for Ronin to somehow get her out of this. General Klein's long fingers are digging into her bicep as they participate in this half-hug it's clear neither of them can stomach. Her hatred for him is easy to understand, but how a father could ever loathe Lily is beyond me.

Instead of giving control of the stage back to Father, Ronin hands it to me. He crosses over and claps me on the shoulder, which I know is a clear message to the people that we do this now. We let vampires touch us. "It's to you, Son," he says, his mouth set in a firm line.

Father motions for me to come stand next to him, but it's too late for that. He's lost hold of the day. He's lost hold of his enemy. He's lost hold of me. So I step forward, declaring who I am and who I'm willing to be for my people, whether or not they respect me for the bitter medicine I'm about to be for them.

I raise my chin with a bland smile for my people. "My fellow fae, in my rescue of Lilya Klein with Prince Salem of Jacoba and Prince Destino of Drexdenberg, I think you cannot blame me for falling hopelessly in love with this beautiful creature. Isn't she stunning?" I pause for their cheers and clapping. When I turn to Lily, all I have to do is extend to her my hand. It's her choice whether or not she takes it, and she practically runs at the offering. She leaves her villain of a father and tucks herself into my side, not hiding behind me, but aligning herself with all that I am, and all we're about to do. She's scared, but she still stand-ing, which is sometimes all life requires of us.

I speak clearly, my grin finally genuine. "I was hoping to present to you my fiancée, but as of last night, I can proudly present to you my bride and yours. We simply couldn't wait another day to be wed, so we eloped. I want to hear the trumpets blasting and people dancing well into the night because the throne is secure! Behold, your future queen!"

The crowd is so wild, I'm not sure they'll ever settle down. This is the greeting she deserves, the accolade my wife should receive for simply existing. Not many can stand in the face of their would-be murderer with grace. Not many would scheme in secret for the betterment of a world that's going to vilify her for her crimes of compassion.

Father's expression is supposed to be joy, but it looks like he's frozen mid-choke. Mother is stunned, her painted lips parted as she gapes at me with what looks like betrayal. I don't think she's upset that I did this, but rather that I stood up to Father without her.

Ronin and Des step to the side so we can bow and wave, showering the crowd with our adoring expressions as the picturesque power couple we are. The fanfare goes on for whole minutes, and I try to trap this image in my mind, because I know in a heartbeat, it will all turn to rage.

Lily's fingers thread through mine. "I want to say some-thing. Can you charm my voice so I can be heard?" she asks while the crowd jumps and cheers for us.

Though the part of me that is my father's son rears up and immediately wants to do all the talking so I can control the spin of the day, a glimmer of hope flickers in my chest when I realize that I am my own man. "Of course, Lily-girl. Whatever you like."

Though I want to shield her from everything, this is her choice. She is strong enough to rule beside me, so I trust her to speak for herself, since up until this point, she's been permitted no voice. I will not mute her passion, as Father's done to my mother.

After I touch Lily's throat and murmur the short string of syllables everybody knows, she rolls back her shoulders to address her people. "Thank you. I'm so honored to be welcomed back. I promise to love you all, as I love Drexdenberg."

The cheering doesn't stop completely, but the waves of questioning expressions ripple outward, and eventually the fanfare quiets so she can speak.

It's happening. The hairs on my arms stand, and I know the nation is about to change.

"When Prince Alexavier found me, I couldn't help my love for him. The same happened when I met Prince Destino of Drexdenberg. So I've married them both." She pauses for the swells of confusion, followed by a mix of nervous laughter and a few cries of outrage. Her hand is shaking against mine but her voice is steady. "One day, I will inherit both crowns. I'll rule with my husbands, and at that time, our territories will be united."

More outrage and less confusion. Salem catches my eye

from his hidden spot at the base of the platform. He nods to lend me his strength, knowing that the tides are quickly turning from cheers to impending rage on a massive scale.

Lily's voice echoes out, her delicate delivery flawless. "I'm so very grateful that King Fairbucks had the foresight to make good on his oversight of the blood shipments. He is too modest to say so, but he goes on and on over our dinners about his love for the vampires, and how he longs to ally our territory with theirs. General Klein has even vowed that no vampire will come to harm at the hands of a fae. If we truly think of ourselves as the superior race, we should not stoop to something as common as greed or violence. Hatred is a plague that makes people ugly."

I love her, playing to their interests. She's incredible.

"I've never met a hateful person who looked attractive. Perhaps that's why we all adore Prince Alexavier, because his love for you and kindness for the shifters and vampires paints him in a heroic light."

Des and I flank her, standing with our chests out and a hand each on her back. This is the moment we'll remember for the rest of our lives. When we're old men, I will remember gripping Des' fingers behind Lily's back so we could stand against a nation too stubborn to change.

Lily leans into our touch, commanding the territory to quiet when she raises her finger. "I've chosen my heroes. It's time for you to do the same. King Ronin, King Fairbucks and General Klein all agree that hatred has done its fair share to make our world ugly. I know you're ready for the fae to lead the way toward the light."

A few brave souls clap, no doubt so turned around that the only thing they can think is to align themselves with whatever the throne says. They may not believe in our cause or even like what we're doing. But those few thousand clapping hands will follow us.

I'll take it.

13

THE NEW WAY OF THINGS

DESTINO

King Fairbucks is livid, which is usually something he feels but doesn't properly express. It mostly comes out in veiled threats and underhanded digs accompanied by manipulation to get you back on his course. But once the festival is underway and the people are properly distracted, he snatches Alex and Lily by their upper arms and jerks them into the palace behind the massive platform, growling at Ronin and me to follow. All of their receiving rooms look the same, what with their ivorum floors, gold-painted walls and furniture too delicate to sit on with any real confidence. Queen Kloe beelines past, announcing to us all that she's been sober long enough.

The General comes in behind us, along with Salem, who I know will never let Lily's father near her without him present. "What's the meaning of this, Fairbucks? A treaty with the vampires? What's next, a tea party with the shifters?"

"It wasn't my idea, and I was strong-armed into it the same moment you were, out in public for the entire territory to see." King Fairbucks launches Lily and Alex forward, content to see them stumble as they find their footing. While Alex looks surprised to be manhandled by his father, Lily is not. I guess Alex still has that "believe the best in people" quality I hope he never loses. I wonder if Lily lost her optimism back when she was eight years old.

Salem growls as he steadies the two, standing behind them to make the entire room aware of his menacing bulk.

The General's nostrils flare. "And you just agreed to it in front of the nation? Now we have to go along with this? Lower the tariffs and make peace with the vampires? I don't even know how that would look!"

Lily finds her footing and her voice first. "It looks like making sure all citizens are on Green Lightning so that no vampire attacks happen and ruin the whole alliance. It looks like owning up to your own words and giving Ronin the blood shipments he's paid for. It looks like marriages similar to mine and Des', which shouldn't have had to happen in secret. It looks like letting the vampires walk around in fae territory without fear of either race being harmed."

Maybe it's because we're alone, with the staff out at the festival, that makes the General think he has permission to lunge at Lily and grab her around the shoulders. Salem, Alex, Ronin and I all dart to intervene, but Salem gets first crack. The General does little more than shake her before he throws her to the ground when Salem knocks the wind from him.

In the span of a breath, Salem has the fae general on his belly on the floor, kneeling on his spine with the man's hands twisted behind his back. It all happens so quickly; I can barely make out how it all happened. General Klein is in his late fifties, while Salem, the shifter army commander, is in his prime. It's not often the two military men even meet face to face. Seeing them in this poetic position, with Salem dominating as only he can, is a sight I would pay to see. I'm so distracted that Ronin beats me to Lily's side.

Ronin pulls up my wife and brushes off her dress, holding her in his arms while she grits her teeth through emotions I can't fathom the depths of. Whatever notion she may have entertained about her father mutating into a good man over the years is now crushed under the weight of this grim reality. Fae men don't put their hands on women. Not when there are witnesses around, at least. The fact that he feels at liberty to throw her around in our presence means he's plotting far worse for when he corners her in private.

I will not let that happen.

Ronin spits on the General's head while he holds Lily tight. His glare connects with King Fairbucks, and it's then I see him fight for his territory. Fight for us. "I will stay long enough to watch you punish General Klein for his assault on the future Queen of Faveda, and the current Princess of Drexdenberg."

Alex's father has the nerve to scoff, and I'm not sure I've ever despised the man more. "I do not intervene on how fathers raise their children. That is not the job of a king."

"*I* am her father, and I demand action be taken against this man!" Ronin thunders, finally drawing a ragged breath from Lily. It's clear she's on the verge of breaking down, but she stands taller in his arms, holding herself back because that's who the world needs her to be in this moment. Ronin snarls down at General Klein. "As Lilya is the future Queen of Drexdenberg, if you do not lock him in your cell, he will be taken to mine to rot for as long as it pleases me. You may not protect your future, but I will."

King Fairbucks pinches the bridge of his nose. "You're honestly behind this? This is what you think is best for the kingdom? That the vampires and fae unite? For what purpose?"

I can't stay quiet any longer. This will be my throne someday, and I am more than capable of fighting for my people. "For the purpose that the vampires don't starve when more blood shipments go suddenly missing. For the purpose of peace, or is that too uncompelling a reason? Are you so very addicted to your small-minded hatred and ignorance?" I move to stand in front of Ronin and Lily. Though I haven't drawn a weapon, my body is tensed and ready to spring into action. "Believe me, Drexdenberg will be horrified at the prospect of uniting with you fae, too. But it's time. I'm tired of watching the world crumble and doing nothing about it. This is the chance to build something real. Something that can stand up against the short-sighted hatred that's keeping the majority stunted and small. The chance to give you more ivorum for your palace and gain a steady supply of blood for my people."

King Fairbucks snarls at me. "I have no need for your people or your silly worldview. Faveda quite sustains itself. For all I care, Drexdenberg can starve and die off, and the world would be a better place."

I point my finger in his direction. "And that is why your days on the throne are numbered, and when you pass on, no one will mourn your death. They will remember you only by your hatred, and will feel sorry for your tiny imagination that cannot fathom peace or kindness."

Alex stands beside me, blocking Lily from view entirely. "Our dungeon or Drexdenberg's, Father. That's the only say you get in this. This man attacked my wife in my presence. The Princess of Faveda is a title that far outstrips the General's. Either you will see to it that order is upheld, or I will. Choose which prison, or I will know you cannot handle the throne any longer."

King Fairbucks crosses the room to get in Alex's face. To his credit, Alex doesn't flinch or even move. Though it's clear King Fairbucks wants his son to feel small, in this moment, Alex looks taller, fierce, and ready for the responsibilities of the throne.

King Fairbucks seethes, all semblance of control lost. "The title of king far outstrips prince or princess. There will be no more strong-arming me like what happened out there on that stage. You will respect my rule, or it will be you in the dungeon."

Ronin's voice picks up from behind me. "You are granted full asylum in Drexdenberg, Son. If your father proves himself a madman who can't see reason, you can live in my castle, under my roof until your father passes on. The whole of Faveda will revolt because they adore you, Alexavier. There is no quicker way to move our plan forward than having it clear your father does not support it."

I'm scrambling to keep up, but I see the glimmer of logic in Ronin's words. Alex is beloved in his homeland. They may not be totally on board with an alliance between Faveda and Drexdenberg yet, but they would storm the castle if Alex was locked inside.

King Fairbucks seems to understand this truth, so he takes a step back, his voice quieting. "What you've done... You have no idea how to rule a kingdom. They are sheep who believe what you tell them. They like being comfortable. They're scared of the outside world, which makes their ivorum towers feel safe."

Alex shakes his head at his father, and suddenly I'm struck with how much more kingly Alex looks than King Fairbucks. More mature, composed. "And that's why the people need me and my way of thinking. I do not believe they are sheep. I know this will be hard because they have been sold hatred and lies for their entire lives. They will not want to change, but because I love them, they must. You do not love them, so you're content to let them chew off their own hands while a people on the other side of our borders suffer." He folds his arms over his chest. "No more. Stay on the throne as long as you like, so long as I get my treaty, and this clown gets locked up." He kicks lightly at General Klein's shoulder, adding insult to injury by marring the spotless white of the man's uniform with the crud on the bottom of his shoe.

King Fairbucks looks lost in his anger, turned around and not in control, which is a rare color on him. He's breathing hard through his nose while the trumpets play happy tunes outside. We all wait in silence while the General cusses in pants and huffs as Salem leans more of his weight on the man's spine to squish the air from his lungs. I swear, I see the corners of Salem's mouth twitch at finally being able to keep Lily's tormentor under his control.

When King Fairbucks finally speaks, his voice is a low boiling kettle, just barely holding back his steaming rage. "Very well. King Ronin, I'll send General Klein to my prison." A collective exhale hits the room while General Klein squirms, his face red. "And as for your treaty, I'll draw something up tomorrow."

"You'll draw up nothing. We'll see General Klein locked in a cell and then *all* of us will come up with a plan that suits all three of our kingdoms in the morning."

"All three?" King Fairbucks says, his head whipping in Salem's direction. "You can't mean you expect the fae to align with the shifters as well."

Ronin slides Lily's hand into mine and steps out from

behind us, his arms at the small of his back as if he's readying to give a lecture in school. "Lily is married to Destino and Alexavier, uniting our territories. She's next going to marry Prince Justice, so when his mother passes on, she will be queen of the three territories, uniting us all."

Lily's hand stiffens in my grip. She shrinks back and steps away. When I turn my head over my shoulder while Ronin and Fairbucks go back and forth, dread fills my belly. We didn't tell her. I forgot to confirm that she knew she wouldn't be marrying Salem, but rather his older brother instead. When I'd made the mistake of assuming she'd marry Salem because I wasn't thinking clearly, I presumed she'd been on the correct train of thought from the beginning. She knows, as well as everyone else does, who the heir to the shifter throne is.

"Lily?" My voice is quiet, so the kings can keep on fighting without her shock being the center display.

"I... Prince Justice is older. Of course. That makes sense. He... I thought... I just assumed... Excuse me." I catch a glimpse of moisture welling in her eyes. For all the parts of me that want to keep her entirely to myself, my chest constricts with pain at the thought of her never getting the chance to be with Salem. It's clear they both want this so very badly, even if they're too afraid to admit it.

Salem's only ever been in love with her, and now he's had to watch his two best friends marry the woman of his dreams. Soon it'll be his brother, if all goes as planned.

Lily backs up and then turns to run when a tear trickles

down her cheek. She's kept her composure so heroically, but this is too much. Even I'm devastated at life's cruelty in keeping the two of them apart.

"Lily, wait!" Salem calls after her, more concerned about our woman than he is about the bloke who's struggling to break free beneath his weight.

"I've got him," I offer. "Alex, give me a hand and find some rope or something." I kneel down on my father-in-law's back, edging Salem out of the way. "Go," I tell him. "Go get her."

Salem shoots me a look of pure panic. "What am I supposed to say?"

For how old Salem's always seemed in my eyes, he looks like a scared boy right now. Despite the rocking world, the corners of my mouth quirk upwards. "Tell her you love her, and then kiss her so beautifully, she forgets your brother's name."

Maybe there's better advice to give my best friend. Something more prudent to our master plan. But at the end of the day, I'm not a ruler. I'm his brother, and I want things for him that maybe fate will be too cruel to give him.

Salem stands, running his hands through his hair before he turns and takes off toward the east wing. Toward his love.

Toward my wife.

14

ALL THIS TIME

LILYA

I'm so stupid. Just beyond hope with how little I thought this whole thing through. I simply assumed I'd be marrying Salem because that's what I wanted. I mean, I didn't *want*-want any of this, but that made the most sense to my hormone-laced brain.

I have two husbands. I don't have space in my life for a crush that's never amounted to anything. Now it's clear to me that whatever fantasies I entertained hold no weight. They can never come true, because I'll be married to his brother, whom I've never met. Never seen. Don't know.

My only relief is that no one saw me break down. I didn't cry through seeing the General again. Didn't lose myself in front of the throngs of people. Didn't devolve into a puddle when the General attacked me and threw me on the ground. Marrying Salem's brother is the thing that's wrecking me, turning me into a mess of emotions when there's work to be done. I should be standing with Lexi and

121

Des, who are my true heroes. I should be reinforcing this treaty between King Fairbucks and Ronin because that's the right thing to do. I should be thanking Salem for intervening when the General roughed me up.

I guess everyone has their breaking point. It's been a while since I met mine. This stupid dress is hard to run in, so I heft up the skirt as I dart up the steps. This dress isn't me. I get the whole matrimonial image thing, but it's also a fae thing, stainless, pure and nearly glowing with light. I'm not that girl, and I feel foolish for pretending so hard that I thought I could trick myself into thinking things could be different, that life could be fair.

But I'm not playing fair. I'm taking two, maybe even three husbands for myself. I'm snatching up whole territories and telling them how to be.

"Lily, slow down!" I hear Salem call from the base of the steps.

I'm halfway up, and there are still so many steps to go. "I'm fine!" I lie, and keep my feet moving. Crying in front of Salem would be the humiliation I can't survive. Especially because he won't understand why. He doesn't love me like that, not how I've loved him for so many years.

I'm the barmaid, nothing more, no matter what this dress declares to the world.

Salem usually doesn't want to be near me, so when I feel the vibrations from his heavy boots swallowing three and four stairs at a time, my pace quickens as much as this dress will allow.

Of course my foot catches on the hem. There are so

many layers of silk to this thing. Of course I trip and fall, smacking my chin on the hard step and clacking my teeth together. I struggle to right myself and scramble away, but Salem catches up to me, because of course he does.

"Are ye so afraid of me tha you'll literally run away?" He's frustrated, not angry when he helps me up and fingers my tender chin.

"I'm not afraid of you," I spout off honestly, forgetting my filter because we're alone, my shin and chin sting, and he's standing so very close. "I've been head over heels in love with you for years! Is that what you want to hear? Do you want to know how pathetic I am that everything in me lights up whenever you came into the pub? How about that I lived for the smallest slice of a moment when my finger brushed yours when I set down your stein of ale? Would it make you happy to know that I never let anyone drink out of your stein because I didn't want anyone else's lips near something that had touched yours?" Tears are streaming down my face, and I'm certain this is the moment I've lost my mind. I'm never this honest, this raw, yet here it is.

Here I am.

I swipe at my cheeks, drying them as best I'm able so my humiliation doesn't drip spots on my dress. "And now I'm supposed to marry your brother, who I don't know, and who isn't you."

He opens his mouth, his whole face filled with such revulsion and confusion that I know I've really stepped in it this time.

I hold up my hand and step back, my butt pressing to

the railing. "I know you don't like fae, and you've never seen me like that. Believe me, I get it. I'll fall in line. I'll marry your brother." I trap a sob in my lungs before it can explode out of me, shaking my head at this whole scene, and the steps that led me here. My hand grips my throat, and when I speak once more, my voice comes out in a whisper. "But going through everything up until this point, seeing the General again, all of it—I can handle the whole mess. On the day I marry your brother and not you, that will be the day I mourn my losses."

Salem's mouth is still open, mute with horror that I ever thought I might have a chance with someone as incredible as him. I know it. I feel the end of my girlish ways cementing in my bones, weighting me down so much that I'll have to cast my silly dreams aside to move on into all I'm supposed to accomplish.

I walk away from him because I know he'll let me go. He doesn't want to be stuck in this conversation, so I release us both from it and trudge up the steps, broken and so very sad.

My door closes behind me, and I can't get my dress off fast enough. It's a lie, the whole thing. That I'm happy, perfect and fae. I pull a knee-length strappy nightgown out of the drawer because I have no intention of leaving this room ever again. I collapse onto Lexi's giant mattress, cover myself with the blanket and let my tears fall freely, not judging a single one of them because they belong to me.

When a knock sounds at the door, I cringe that Salem

isn't the kind of guy who can let this mess go and pretend it never happened. That would be the best-case scenario. Who would've guessed that the man who doesn't like to talk about anything won't do me the kindness of looking the other way when I'm clearly wallowing in my own humiliation?

"No, thank you," I call over my shoulder. "I'll see you all in the morning."

"I'm coming in," Salem announces like a threat. I open my mouth to protest, but Salem stalks into the room, closing the door behind him. At least my shame is limited to just us. "Ye love me?" Salem asks, his voice rough.

"No," I spout, my attitude in full swing. "I just like to say that to random men and then burst into tears."

He rips the comforter off of me, startling a squeak from my lips. He doesn't look angry; he looks untamed, his eyes wide and his nostrils flared.

I sit up with a scowl as I push the skirt of my night-gown down to make sure my thighs are covered. "Can I help you?"

Salem looks truly worried, confused that the world's thrown him this curve he can't possibly want to catch. "Did Des make ye say those things? Alex?"

"Huh? Of course not."

"Tha's really ye? Tha's what you've been thinking about me all this time?"

"Would you get out of here? I don't want to talk about this with you another second. At least have the decency to pretend it never happened!"

Salem sits on the foot of the bed, his long legs over the edge while he leans his elbows on his thighs and pushes his hands through his shortened hair. His face is washed with an intensity that stills my movements until a quietness falls over us both.

When he speaks, his voice is so low that I have to lean in to hear him. "Five years ago during the full moon of the fifth month, I'd been in a bad fight. My men had lost a battle with the fae army, and we were still licking our wounds. I never take time off, unless it's to visit Alex and Des once a month. After hanging with them for a day, I didn't want to go home. So I wandered into Neutral Territory. Into your pub."

It's not what I expect him to say. I mean, it's so very specific. I'm not sure I've ever heard him string so many sentences together at once.

When I don't speak, Salem continues. "There weren't supposed to be any fae in Neutral Territory, but there ye were. Purple hair and prettier than anyone has a right looking after my people took such a bad beating. I sat down in your pub and ye asked me what I wanted to drink. I was so mad at ye. For no reason, of course. I was mad at any fae who could look me in the eye after all your people had done to mine. Maybe I ordered. Maybe ye just brought me a drink. I can't remember. But ye said I looked like no one had been kind to me in about a hundred years." He pauses and swallows hard. "Then ye brought me some water and a napkin, and scrubbed the dried blood off my knuckles for me."

He brings his hand down and flexes it a few times, as if seeing the blood all over again.

Then he clears his throat. "It was the nicest thing anyone other than the lads had done for me in a long time. Then ye smiled like it was all no big deal and refused to charge me for my drink." He shakes his head.

"I don't remember that at all. The first time I saw you was five years ago, yes. But you weren't injured. You came in and ordered an ale. Barely looked at me, but I couldn't keep myself from staring at you."

"Staring at me?"

I nod slowly. "I thought you were the most beautiful man I'd ever seen. So still. So regal. You carry yourself like... I don't know. There's just something about you. When you walk into a room, I'm sure other things are happening, but I can't remember them." It's a stupid thing to say, but apparently I have no pride anymore.

He shakes his head as he rubs the nape of his neck. Is he blushing? "I was wearing my cloak with my hood covering my face the first time I came in. Ye looked after my cuts when ye didn't even know who I was?"

"I had no idea. I don't even remember doing it. I mean, it was five years ago."

"I didn't know what to do with the idea tha any fae other than Alex could be good to a shifter. So I came back a month later to see if ye were only nice to shifters when ye felt sorry for us. Tha must be the day you're thinking was the first time ye saw me." He reaches into the breast pocket of his military shirt and pulls out a stack of napkins, lain flat against each other in perfect order. "I took one of these to mark every visit. Wrote down anything ye said to me, along with the date. This is only part of the stack. The rest is back home in my safe." He hands them to me without looking in my direction.

I leaf through them, my brows furrowing. "I don't understand. Is this you spying on me to see if I'm trying to trick you or something? You're cataloging what I say so you can prove that… what? That I'm just as awful as the fae soldiers who hurt you?"

He still can't look at me, so he stares at his hands, his elbows resting on his knees. "Nothing like tha. I was curious at first, and then I was… I'm not sure what the word for it is." He swallows hard, his fingers tightening and loosening over and over. "I just wanted to hear your voice. Wanted to make sure I got it right when I went back home and replayed your little mannerisms in my head."

I'm completely still, except for the thrumming of my curious heart. "I don't understand."

"I've been in love with ye for five years, Lily. I just knew ye could never love a shifter, so I kept my distance."

There are no words. No coherent ones, anyway. I leaf through the napkins, my eyes widening at his tight scrawl that's all caps. "'What can I get you to drink?' is on practically all of these. Man, I'm generic." My eyes flick over maudlin waitress statements like, "Would you like a refill?" "Can I get you anything else?" "Are you hungry tonight?" I hold up the next napkin, dated from two years ago. "This one was supposed to be sexy, but it looks lame on a napkin."

It's the only way I can get Salem to look in my direction. He nods after scanning his handwriting. "It was sexy." His gray eyebrows tent, perplexed. "All this time, ye really wanted me?"

I nod, handing him back the napkins. Our fingers touch, as they have so many times over the years when I'd set down his stein before him.

I don't know why that's it, but the confusion dies in my soul in that instant, and all I feel is need. All the times I denied myself what I truly wanted swarm around the room, muting out all the reasons why this can't work, why we shouldn't go in for that second touch.

His lips are on mine in the next breath, and all I can think is that this is the one man I've wanted for no reason other than pure need.

I need him, and so I take him.

15

SO VERY MINE

LILYA

*T*here's no politics in our kiss, no plan. It's a mess, and so are we. The introduction to this new phase of our lives is given only a cursory greeting before the panic that this might get snatched away drives us to deepen each kiss, make each touch count. Light caresses turn to manhandling, and I honestly can't tell if I'm being rougher with him or if his hands are gripping me in the best kind of too-tight way.

I've kissed exactly two men my entire life, but my body knows what it wants, even if it doesn't know how to get there. I find my way to straddling his lap on the edge of the bed. Whether he draws me there or my legs part of their own accord, I can't say. My fingers fumble with the buttons of his military shirt, needing more of him, always more. His body is warm, and I love how very hairy he is.

Salem's chest is broad and thick, begging me to memorize every inch of it with my hands. I press him down across the mattress, his eyes going from wide to lidded when my thumb trails across his nipple. "All this time..." he asks, his voice ragged as his hips buck into me.

My thighs clamp down, holding on for the ride I never dreamed I'd be so lucky to enjoy. "We could've been doing this in the storage closet of the pub for years," I snigger, and then meet his lips when his chin jerks toward me, inviting me to kiss him more, harder. "Tell me this is what you want."

I love his growl, and swallow it down greedily when it passes between our hungry mouths. He bites down on my lower lip, and I'm fairly certain I've never wanted anything more in my life than this man. This kiss. It's surreal, the whole thing. I worry I'm dreaming, that I've wanted him so badly, I'm hallucinating the life I crave.

But he tastes so real, so very mine.

His hands are large and calloused, rough as he grips the backs of my thighs and trails his thumbs upward over the layers of silk. His lips claim me with a fervor that makes me feel both brazenly bold and simultaneously shy. The bristle of his facial hair on my skin makes me feel alive, like I've been asleep for so long, and now this beautiful mountain is finally mine for the taking. It's too good to be true, so I close my eyes and give in to the dream, hoping it never comes to an end.

Salem flips the hem of my nightgown over my backside and kneads my butt, his fingers dipping under the fabric of my underwear in intervals I can't predict and desperately need. All I can do is hold on and kiss him harder, telling him that I want his hands exactly there. Exactly everywhere.

He rolls us over so he's on top, and I reach for his belt, eager for all that he is. "Wait," he breathes, and it's then I realize he's panting, his eyebrows stitched together with fear. "I need... Give me a second. Something feels off. When shifters get overexcited, they can..." He shakes his head. "I don't want to shift in the middle of... I'm not sure if tha's what's happening, but something feels strange."

My arms find their way around his neck, inviting him to lay atop me, crushing me into the mattress under his massive weight. His breathing is ragged and unsteady, which I take as a compliment. I don't exactly have much experience with this sort of thing. My body just knows that it wants Salem, so parts of it gravitate to his touch.

"Strange?" I question. "I was hoping you were feeling good, not strange."

He has the wherewithal to chuckle into my hair. "More than good. But something's building in my chest. Like a heart attack I really want to happen." He shakes his head and then kisses me. "I'm not explaining it right. Feels like the first time I shifted when I was younger." His kisses connect us in pitters and patters of pleasure mixed with peace. "It's good. Very good. Just more intense than I ever knew something like this could be. My body's trying to figure itself out."

Even as he's trying to calm himself, we sneak in kisses that are exchanges of affection and reassurance. But after only a handful, they come like a tidal wave, rocking us both out to sea, and so very far from the safety of the shore. I cling to his neck as I'm swept away, trusting that he'll be there to anchor me when life has other plans.

He kisses me like I'm the only woman in the world. His eyes are scrunched like his joy is causing him actual physical pain.

My leg coils around his, trapping it and keeping it as my treasure. Salem groans as his pelvis sinks into mine, rocking us both with pangs of pleasure and permanence. All this time, he's wanted me. All this time, I could've been his.

My nightgown rides up, and his fingers find their way to trace a heated line up the top of my thigh, scorching me so it feels like my whole body burns for him. When his thumb loops in the band of my underwear, heat shoots through me from my hip all the way through my legs, pushing my knees further apart.

His eyes are still scrunched like he's in agony, grunting and groaning through the undulations of desire he's pressing between my legs. When I manage to unhook his belt, he lets out a bleat of fear. "Lily, don't let me shift!"

My hands take on a new purpose, derailing my mission to get him naked as soon as possible. Instead I trail my fingers up and down his broad back, loving the feel of his tufts of silver hair bristling across my nails. "It's okay," I reassure him. "Nothing bad's going to happen. It's just you and me. Whatever shifter craziness is going on in your body, I'm not afraid of it. If you shift, it doesn't ruin anything." He's breathing like he's in the middle of running from a monster, so I kiss his nose and gaze adoringly up at him. This man has mattered to me for so very long. When I open my mouth, my words hold no hesitation. "I love you, Salem."

His breathing slows as he takes in the scope of my affection for him. He brings his hand up to trace the curve of my cheek. "I have loved ye for so very long. You're it for me. Since the first time I met ye, I haven't so much as looked at another woman."

My mouth draws to the side. "You stood back and let Des and Lexi marry me. I don't understand."

His gray eyes are filled to the brim with light and sincerity. Though the lamp gives the room a subtle amount of brightness, it feels like Salem's eyes are the only stars in the universe. "I was certain ye would never lower yourself to be with a shifter, but I wanted ye safe. It killed me to see the men at the bar leer at ye. So when Alex came up with the marriage idea, I suggested ye because I knew ye would be good to Des, and Des would keep ye safe. If I couldn't have ye, I at least wanted to be sure ye didn't end up with a man I'd have to gut in his sleep for being disrespectful."

My eyes widen at his declaration. "I honestly had no idea you liked me at all." I steal a second to kiss him again, since it's clearly been too long since I've tasted his full lips. "I thought I was a tricky fae to you, that you hated me. You barely talked to me at all. Froze every time I touched you."

"I was trying not to say something stupid. Nervous, I guess."

My thumb traces the delicious arches of his upper lip.

I've seen myself do this so many times in my imagination; it's surreal to be able to act on the urge. "Are you nervous now?"

His chin moves from left to right. "Terrified."

"Then let's go slower."

When he kisses me this time, the rhythm is steadier, measured and more purposeful. There's no harried grabbing. My nails take their time appreciating the spiky quality of the freshly-cut hairs in back. He smells like the woods, and I love it. I want to roll around just like this in the grass with him, taking our time and letting nature cradle our trembling limbs.

"It's happening again," he warns me. "Tha happy heart attack feeling."

"Should we stop?" *Please don't tell me to stop. I'm fairly certain I might cry.*

The corner of his mouth drags upward. "Never." Another kiss, and another. "Ye won't be frightened if I shift in the middle of all this?"

"I love your wolf. I'm not sure why you think anything about you might put me off. It's you I want. All of you."

I love his low growl, and devour the sound that vibrates my lips. His moans of contentment begin to mutate further and further into pangs of worry, building with more distress after every few kisses. I let him control the pace, and he seems to want to keep going through the pain of whatever's happening inside of him.

Then something switches—a turn of the air that pushes him to speed up, embracing the heart attack that fuels him to kiss me deeper, his tongue parting my lips. His fingers don't just tangle in my hair, they grip and pull, jerking a strangled noise of ecstasy from my lips as he kisses his way down my throat. "Salem! Honey, I need you. More!" I'm demanding as my body arches for him, giving him access to whatever parts of me please his roving hands.

"It's happening!" he shouts, fear laced in between his cries of desire.

His whole body heats up, nearly too hot to touch. My hands fall away. "Salem?"

His head jerks back and he howls—a purely wolf sound while he's still wholly man. I don't understand it, and by the looks of the panic on his face, neither does he. He's suddenly sweating, and I'm starting to worry that maybe he is having a heart attack. I've seen him shift before, and it's nothing like this.

His back bows so he's propping his upper half a few feet angled away from me, like he's readying to address the ceiling. "It's trying to get out of me. Take it!"

"Take what?"

It's then I see it. A ball of light is calling out to me, glowing from his bare chest like something too spectacular for this world to quantify. I touch it, and my hand bounces away, the heat too much for my fingers to be near.

"It's burning!" he shouts, breathing through his teeth.

"What is it?"

He shakes his head, clawing at the mattress on either side of my head. "I don't know, but it wants to belong to ye. Get it out!"

"How?"

Before the next breath finds me, his mouth descends on mine. The ball of heat burns my chest as it climbs up through his body, along his throat and makes its way into his mouth.

My lips part, his tongue strokes mine, and I take the thing that's causing him so much agony. Whatever it is, I'll endure it so he doesn't have to. I'm scared but certain I'll do whatever I have to so Salem isn't hurting any longer.

But the second it slides from his mouth into mine, the inferno quiets to a cozy purr, warming me like a pleasant evening by the fireplace. "There. That wasn't so bad. You feel any better?"

Salem's answer is to pass clean out on top of me, all breath leaving the both of us in a gust. I manage to slide him to the side so he's only half atop me, which suits us both just fine.

The warmth I've swallowed from him envelops me from head to toe, filling my insides and painting every wrong thing in the world with an ethereal light.

Salem's here, so I find that I'm not as bothered by the General's presence in the palace. I'm not worried about how we're going to unite the three territories.

In fact, with Salem's breath caressing my cheek, I find I can't bring myself to worry about anything at all.

My eyes close, finally feeling like I'm home.

16

ATTACHED

SALEM

I have to pee, but tha would also mean I need to get up. I don't want to move. This amazing dream is better than all the others, and when I open one eye, I see tha it's real. She's here, sleeping soundly beside me. Her deep breathing is so soothing, I could fall asleep all over again.

Except I really do have to pee.

The washroom's only a handful of steps away, but the only part of me tha is kind of okay with parting from her is my bladder, which can't be ignored much longer.

I move the bed too much with my bulk, but do my best not to wake her. Each footstep tha takes me away from her feels all wrong. I relieve myself and then decide tha if I'm going to be with Lily, I should bathe as often as the fae do. She might be expecting tha. I turn on the water and step under the spray, exhaling at the luxury. Showering isn't something shifters normally can do, but I suppose I could convince Alex to meet me at the border to spray me down each time I come to see her. I want Lily's nose buried in the crook of my neck. I want her to love waking up smelling like me.

I dry off, pull on my jeans and lay back down beside her under the covers, sighing as the small part of me tha felt carved out and missing when distance was put between us is finally filled again.

She's real. It happened. I woke up to Lily, and she's going to wake up to me.

Is tha what she wants? The thought hits me in vibrations of panic, but they're put to rest the moment she turns in her sleep and digs her hand under the comforter, sliding her fingers to rest over my abdomen. The little "mm" noise she makes coats my heart like honey.

I'm what she wants.

Her nightgown rides up as her leg coils around mine, claiming my right leg without apology.

Take it. My whole body is yours to do with as ye please.

Tha thought makes me still. I don't know where it came from. It's not untrue, but the intensity with which it strikes me gives me pause.

Something's different. Not wrong, exactly, but strange.

"Is it morning?" she murmurs, her breath teasing my nipple.

"Only if ye wish it."

She laughs airily through her nose. "I'm starving. Can we ignore the rest of the world and eat without having to bother with it being morning?"

I chuckle as I kiss her, already angling my body to sit up. "I'll bring ye up some breakfast, so ye don't have to deal with anyone."

"No, no," she yawns, sitting up beside me. "I'm being a baby. I'm up."

"Go get ready for the day, then. I'll have breakfast ready for ye by the time you're finished."

She opens her mouth to protest, but then shakes her head. "It might take me some time to get used to this. Thanks, Salem. That's real decent of you."

I kiss her lips before I go, knowing tha she is the best flavor in the world. The moment she vanishes inside the washroom, I pull on my shirt, socks and boots and trot down the stairs. Tha void I felt earlier when we were parted by the span of a few feet comes back, growing more disconcerting with every step I take away from her. Jays, what's wrong with me?

She needs to eat. I'm being ridiculous.

The fae kitchen isn't usually a place I'm comfortable in, but then again, tha's true about most of this place. Everything's shiny and spotless, and I'm the big oaf who comes in with mud on his boots. The cook doesn't greet me, but pretends I'm invisible, moving deftly around me without making eye contact, which suits us both just fine. I rummage around for a couple of apples, some icing-laced sweet rolls left over from last night's festival we largely skipped out on, and a bowl of nuts. Then I set to squeezing her some orange juice.

I need to get back up there. If she slips and falls in the

tub, what will my excuse be? I was juicing an orange? I'm not accustomed to this level of awareness. I'm suddenly conscious of every single danger tha could befall my Lily.

My Lily.

I'm caught in the debate between which is more perilous—the possibility of her cracking her head on the side of the tub if she slips, or her coming down with some illness because she doesn't have enough Vitamin C.

I shake off my worry, wondering what in the blazes has gotten into me. "Is there a tray I can use?" I ask the cook, who hisses as if I've said something offensive. Fae are the worst.

The cook yanks a tray from the cabinet under the island in the center of the kitchen and thwaps it on the butcher block, unable to speak to me or look in my direction.

Grand.

It feels good to take care of my woman like this. To give her something she needs. With every step I take back to her, tha ball of restless anxiety in my chest begins to settle. Everything unbuttoned inside of me clicks back into place.

When I reach Alex's bedroom, my grin fades when I hear Alex and Des talking with Lily from inside. It's inevitable tha I can't have her all to myself, but it was a grand fantasy while it lasted.

"It's a partial win," Alex assures her.

Lily's voice is controlled, with none of the passion between the sheets we shared last night. "I appreciate you fighting so hard to get your father to budge on anything. I don't know what the General has on your father, but it must be something big if he resisted carrying out the law this badly."

Alex's voice sounds surprised. "You really think there's something deeper here? I assumed it was just Father not wanting to be wrong."

I move into the room, and her whole demeanor lights up at the sight of me. I mean, me. "Did you really bring me breakfast?"

"Aw, you shouldn't have, brother." Alex grins and reaches for one of the apples. I block his hand from taking any of my woman's food and set the tray on the bed. She's already showered and dressed in a white gown that hangs to just above her knees. It doesn't have sleeves, and looks like the kind of dress fae women wear when they're on the beach.

"I'll bite your paws if ye touch this tray, ye greedy mongrel. It's for Lily and me."

"Speaking of you and Miss Lily," Des says with a tease in his voice. "Alex tells me he came into his room last night to find some shifter in his bed with his wife. Funny, that."

"We understand each other now," I say simply. If they need more explanation, they're not going to get it from me. They know what's going on. They know I've been smitten with her for a long time.

Lily runs a brush through her damp hair tha's more purple than lavender when it's wet. She casts a wary look to the guys. "I hope that's okay."

Des grins at her. "What? Is there something sordid going on that you'd like to share with the group?"

Lily's eyes narrow and the brush stills in her curls. "Not particularly. The three of you are… I can't explain it. So I won't."

Alex stands between us, which is not where I prefer him. "Did the two of you have sex on my bed? Because that's the kind of thing I'd like to have been there for."

She gapes at him, like she's never had a dirty thought in her life. "Lexi, you know we did no such thing."

"No such thing? So, not even kissing?"

Her cheeks flame pink, and even though she's squirming as she tries to slap a voice to the truth, I can't bring myself to put her out of her misery. I want to hear tha she's not ashamed of us. Of me.

"Well, there might've been kissing." Her jaw firms as she glowers at Alex and Des. "And being that Salem didn't tease either of you about kissing me, I'm sure you'll both be gentlemen and won't pester him about it."

"Oh, you're certain you've married gentlemen, are you?" Des teases.

I pick up an apple and put it in her hand the second she sets down her hairbrush. "Ye should eat."

She takes a bite and then motions to the tray. "So should you. Are you feeling any better? Last night was intense. Are you alright?"

I know she's talking about me having to pause everything so I didn't shift atop her, and then completely passing out. I take a bite of the second apple to appease her worry tha I'll waste away. "Best I've ever been. I'll get my wolf under control."

Des leans over her shoulder and takes a crunch out of her apple. "What happened, brother? Performance anxiety?"

I want to punch Des in his smug face. "Nothing like tha. We were kissing, and I almost shifted. It was strange. Like I couldn't control it. I'm not sure what happened." I don't know how to explain tha a ball of lava formed in my chest, came out of my mouth and slid down her throat, so I skip it, which seems to suit Lily just grand, because she doesn't bring up the odd point.

Alex claps me on the back. "Overexcited, eh? That's not surprising. She's quite a woman."

Lily folds her hands before her, looking downward modestly at the compliment. "Thanks, guys." Then she waves off the moment, taking another bite of her apple after she pecks Des' cheek.

Tha's fine. Why wouldn't it be fine? She kisses Des all the time. Then why can't I brush away the sight? I shouldn't mind it, and don't want to admit to myself tha I do.

King Ronin strolls in, his shoulders back and looking like he's never missed a night of sleep in his life. His hair is perfectly combed and his trousers are pressed, which makes me wonder if tha's something I should care about.

I've never been particularly fond of Ronin, but when he greets my Lily with a hug and kisses both her cheeks, my vision changes.

Red. The scene is painted in red. My hackles are raised and my heart is racing. He shouldn't touch her. Has no right to be tha close.

My apple drops to the floor as I lunge in the vampire king's direction, shifting mid-jump to knock him out of the way. I'm not satisfied until his back hits the floor.

17

GRAND

SALEM

Ronin shouts his shock, holding his hands up to display his innocence while I growl over his supine form. "Steady, Salem! It was only a greeting."

My snarl is loud, and doesn't stop until Lily drops to her knees beside me. Then I'm a puppy, my tail hooking around her leg as she leads me away from Ronin. "Hey, it's alright. That's just how Ronin and I are with each other. It doesn't mean anything other than friendship. Easy, pup." Her fingers in my fur are just about the best feeling in the world. I sit before her, equal parts guarding and enjoying her touch.

Ronin stands slowly, brushing off his clothes. "Odd. Did I miss something? Did I offend you, darling?"

Lily shakes her head. "Of course not. I'm always glad to see you. Salem, what's going on?"

I turn into a man on my knees, and I feel no shame as I wrap my arms around her middle, bringing her head to rest against my chest as we kneel together on Alex's floor. Better. Tha's much better. I'm calmer now, my insides less rattled. Jays, I feel manic, completely beside myself with worry tha I've turned into a man without reason. "I don't know what's wrong with me." I want to say more, but I feel too many eyes on me, so I turn and curve my upper lip at them. Des and Alex know I want to be by myself, so they move for the door.

Ronin freezes, his eyes calculating my every move. "Destino, Lily could use a glass of water. Could you get it for her?"

Before Des can move to the bathroom to pour her some water, I'm on my feet. "I'll get it." I'm already moving toward the door, making sure I beat Des to it. He doesn't need to get my woman water. I do tha. Like I don't know when my woman's thirsty.

Ronin tsks Lily. "Did you stub your toe, dear?"

I'm by her side in the next second, hefting her off her feet and setting her on the edge of the bed. Her eyes are wide and she's protesting tha she did no such thing, but she's always pretending like everything's grand when I know she's bothered. Not on my watch. I kneel before her and pry at each of her toes, testing them for tenderness and making sure there aren't any visible marks or abrasions on them. I don't see anything, but one can never be too careful. "Alex, she needs to see a healer. A female healer. Can ye call one to come up here? She shouldn't be walking."

Alex's voice sounds wary, and not like he's taking this seriously. "You alright, Lily-girl?"

Lily runs her fingernails through my hair, and I'm instantly purring for her. "I didn't stub my toe, guys. And even if I did, I hardly think that calls for a trip to a healer. I'm really fine, Salem. Honest."

I'm not sure I believe her. "The healer will decide if you're okay. Alex, call the healer."

Visions of her feet falling clean off plague my mind. I warm them with my hands, blowing on her toes and rubbing the soles to soothe whatever ache might still be lingering. Her lips part and her lashes flutter because *I* give her pleasure. *I* relax her.

Ronin holds up his hand to stop Alex. "No need, Alexavier. I was testing a theory. I admit, I'm not as familiar with Salem as you boys are. Is this sort of behavior normal?"

Alex and Des both shake their heads, ignoring my growl. Des folds his arms over his chest. "I mean, we've known he's got it bad for our girl, but he's never been like this with her or anyone. Is he touched in the head or something?"

Ronin nods, and I fight back the urge to punch him. I blow on her toes again, rubbing her heels until a contented sigh escapes her lips. I love tha sigh. I want to chase it and capture it so I can stare at it whenever it pleases me.

"Salem, sit down, Son," Ronin says to me.

I obey, but only because I'm almost sitting as it is, so I turn and plop down on my butt, draping her leg over my shoulder so I can continue rubbing it.

Ronin grabs a chair and drags it over to us, sitting down

and leaning forward, like he's about to deliver some holy truth. His voice comes out quiet and respectful, which makes me hate him a wee bit less. "Did you two have sex last night?"

Lily's leg angles across my chest, like she's trying to protect me from the question tha's frankly none of the king's business. "No. We kissed."

More than kissed, I want to say, but I don't have the gall to correct her in public. "We connected. We belong to each other now."

"Is that so?" Alex comments, his voice casual and conversational as he leans against Ronin's chair on the left side. "Because I thought the whole marriage thing meant that Des and I belong to her."

I shrug because what Lily and I have is just as permanent as a marriage.

Ronin motions me forward. "I want to look in your eyes, Son. Can I do that?"

My first instinct is to protest, but Lily moves her leg from my grip, nudging me to bend toward him, so I obey her unspoken wish. Ronin shows me his hands before he touches the skin beneath my eyes, peering inside for barely a blink before he lets out a low moan of despair. "Oh, no. Salem, what have you done?"

I lean back and tug at Lily's leg, feeling loads better with its dainty weight draped across my chest. I massage her calf now, and her hand finds its way into my hair.

I love her. Oh, I love her. She touches me like she's not afraid to.

Ronin runs his hand over his face, looking like he's a mix of exhausted and exasperated. "It shouldn't be possible, but it's happening."

"What?" Des asks, standing on Ronin's right.

"I've never seen a shifter with anything other than gray eyes, have you?"

Des leans in closer. "No. What are… Salem doesn't have… Oh! How did you do that, brother?"

Des is staring at me, gaping like I've done something shocking. I hold Lily's leg tighter. "How'd I do what?"

Alex swears. "One of your eyes is blue! Fae blue. That's not possible. And the other is darker gray. Des, isn't it darker?"

Des nods, his mouth dropped open.

Ronin sits back in his seat, his palms running over his slacks as he shoots Lily a worried look. "A shifter's eyes go from a light gray to a dark gray when they're mated. Like they're taking on a portion of the other's strength and adding it to their own. The first ever blue-eyed shifter?"

Alex's eyes bulge as he steps toward us. "Tell me you didn't! It's not possible! You can't have mated with her!" Then he steps back, as if I've shoved him or something. "You mated with my wife the day after I married her?"

My face sours. "It wasn't like tha. I can't mate with her. She would have to be a shifter. My wolf can't mate with a fae. Tha's ridiculous."

Ronin's gaze stays fixed on me. "Does Lily look feverish?"

"What?" I'm on my feet, my hands on her shoulders to

gently lay her down on the bed. I touch her forehead with the back of my hand, but I don't feel any heat. "No fever right now, but ye can't be too careful. Alex, where is tha healer? A cool cloth. Hold on, pup."

The second I step away, she sits up. "Salem, Ronin's wrong. I'm not feverish. I'm not sick at all."

"The healer will tell us if ye are. I'm not taking chances." I cross the room and pour her a glass of water, then wet a washrag, wringing it out before coming back to her bedside and folding her fingers around the cup. While she sips, I dab the rag on her forehead, her cheeks and the nape of her neck. I run it down her arms and shins, just to be safe. She protests the entire time, promising she's not sick, but I'm incapable of letting something like tha go.

Alex swears again, his hand on his forehead.

"What are ye so worked up about?" I make the mistake of asking.

"You mated with our wife! How are we supposed to get around that? How are we going to actually be with her when you're mated? Have you ever known a shifter who allowed another man near his mate? It's insane, your bond. And now you've gone and done the impossible. Undo it!" he shouts like a wee baby.

I narrow my eyes at him. "I know she's your wife. I was there for both weddings. Jays, I'm not delusional."

Des steps toward her. "Oh, really? Then how about I give my wife a kiss? That should be fine, yeah?"

A band in my chest tightens, and my hackles raise, but I

muscle through my gut instinct. "Why wouldn't tha be fine?"

Lily's been practically mute this entire time, but when she speaks, her words whip at my chest. "Then kiss me, Des. Salem, this should be okay, right?"

"Right. Go ahead." Though as I say the words, I hate them. She's clearly mine.

Des approaches and lifts her hand, making her stand when she should be sitting down, at the very least. If she has a fever on top of stubbing her toe, standing seems like playing with fire. Des holds her cheek, angling her toward me so I can see the entire thing—her willingness and his desire for my woman.

My mate.

I flinch at the word tha comes to me clearly, but feels like it's out of nowhere.

I've never begrudged Des anything. He's closer to me than my own brother. But watching Lily's eyes flutter shut as her lips mold to his is a slow torture I'm unprepared for. My wolf is in agony, howling for the pain to stop.

"Enough!" I roar, shocked at the fervor in my voice. Alex and Des flinch at my volume, but it's Lily's yelp and jump backward tha brings me back to myself. I scared her. I scared my woman.

My hand moves to my chest to stem whatever tha was. Pain? Tension? Anger? I'm not sure.

"Clouds on earth, Salem!" Alex stands between me and the two of them, as if I'm going to pounce and tear apart my own best friend.

I won't. Parts of me are tempted, but it's still Des. I would never hurt him. I'm not sure I'm capable.

Ronin introduces calm to the room just when I feel I might panic myself into a fit of some sort. "At least we know what we're dealing with. We can work with this. Alexavier, Destino, this might be far more complex a relationship than you bargained for, but it's not the end of everything. Salem, you're going to have to learn to control your urges. It's good for Lily to be with Alexavier and Destino. This was the plan. This is what she wants, so you can't take it from her."

He's right. I hate when Ronin's right, because he gets so smug about it, but I can't deny the facts. "Ye want Des and Alex?" I need to hear her say out loud tha this is what she wants, so I can want it for her.

She looks almost apologetic, and I hate tha I'm doing this to her. "I do. I love them. I love you. And even if those things weren't true, we've still got a job to do. Our marriages are the only way to unite the territories. That's bigger than all of it." She owns her words, her chin tilting up, unembarrassed that we've bucked all conventions.

"Then tha's what I want for ye. I'll get myself under control. Ye can keep us all. This won't be a bad thing," I promise. "I'll make sure I'm never a bad thing for ye."

Her feet scamper towards me, and everything in my bones sings when she crashes into my arms. "Thank you. I'm so sorry. I didn't know that could happen!"

"Me neither." I can't help but chuckle. "Oh, man. I'm mated. Never thought I'd see the day."

Alex leans against the wall, the back of his head banging against the hard surface over and over. "Fantastic. Never mind how hard this is going to make our relationship. We'll figure it out somehow. But she's supposed to marry your brother. That's the whole point of this—to unite the kingdoms with her as the queen. I highly doubt you'll be okay with her marrying old Justice Butcher now."

My wolf doesn't snarl but cuts right to the bark. The vicious sound rattles around inside of me, though my lips stay shut until I can find the right words. Or the wrong ones. I'm not sure. "No. No, ye can't marry Justice. His hands on ye? No. I saw your face. Ye told me ye didn't want to marry him."

"I don't," she admits. "I'm sorry, guys. As much as I'm in this, I didn't put it together that I wouldn't be marrying Salem. I didn't realize the plan was for me to attach myself to his brother. I can't do it. I have my limits, and that's the line I can't cross." She holds out her hand to Des, who comes right to her but hesitates before touching her fingers. His eyes check with mine, waiting for my curt nod before he kisses her cheek and loops his littlest finger through hers.

This is okay. This is normal. She wants this. I'm to share her affections. Des is a good man. Grand. It's all grand. I'll make it grand, so help me.

"I love you, Des. Maybe it didn't start out like that, but I grew into it." Then she extends her other hand to Alex, who kicks himself off the wall and strolls over to her, faking ease like a true fae. "And I didn't have a chance at not loving you, Lexi. Please stay with me while we figure this out."

Alex's shoulders lower, the hardness in his eyes softening around the edges. "Hey, of course we'll stay. 'Til death parts us, right? That's what we agreed on." He shakes his head at the both of us. "I knew how bad Salem had it for you. If this whole situation didn't have the mating thing factored in, I would be nothing but happy for you two." Alex kisses her forehead and pulls her a few inches from me so her head is resting against his chest. Alex shoots me a look of warning when he can see my discomfort at being parted from her growing more noticeable on my features. The pain compounds at the sight of her in another man's arms, but I bear it.

"It's grand. All grand," I say as I breathe through my nose in long drags, talking my wolf down and reminding us both tha this is what Lily wants. This is good for her. More people to keep her safe.

Alex trails his hand up and down Lily's back. She seems to like it, so I hold myself back. "Easy, Lily-girl. Marrying Justice wasn't even in the plan when you married Des. If the farthest you're willing to go is marrying two of us and mating yourself with the third, that's more than any other woman would do for the territories. You don't need to marry Justice. If you become queen of two territories and remain a princess of the third, that'll still work."

"It's not as much power as we wanted her to have," Ronin reminds us, as if we're unaware. "It might work, but there's equal chances it won't because she won't have real decision-making power to affect the Jacoba throne."

Des places his hand on her back. "Then the four of us will have to fix the mess together. It's unfair for us to put saving all three territories on Lily's shoulders. Alex is right. She won't marry Justice. Frankly, even if this whole thing with Salem hadn't happened, I still might've suggested abandoning that part of the plan. I can't handle it."

Alex bumps his fist to Des. "Me neither." Then he reaches out to bump my fist, and I have the control to participate without punching him clear across the face for holding her for this long.

Grand. It'll all be grand.

18

NEW QUEST

ALEXAVIER

It's a full day and night that we hole ourselves in my bedroom before anyone comes to break us out of our seclusion. We need space to figure out how to make this work without the constant fear that Salem's going to make our lives miserable. It's kissing my wife with my best friends watching every move, sucking the romance out of the whole act. But I understand this is temporary. We need to build up a rhythm so we're not quite as on-edge. I kiss Lily while Des watches Salem, who's breathing through his nose like a beast and holding himself back as best he can. He hasn't attacked, so that's good, but it's clear the urge is there.

Ronin left for Drexdenberg yesterday after we firmed up the trade agreement, so that's taken the tension down a notch. It seems Salem can tolerate Des and I holding, kissing and caressing Lily, but Ronin hugging her is on the edge of too much. Though Ronin voiced his desire to stay, in the interest of keeping his head attached to his shoulders, we insisted he leave so we had the space to adjust to the intensity of Salem's bond with Lily.

We're exhausted but I can see progress. I truly believe we can find a way to make this work. And somewhere in the back of my mind, I'm a little happy it's all coming together like this. It's not ideal, and definitely not how we planned it, but now I'm permanently tied to my two best friends whom I've had to meet with in secret for years. We get to live together, rule together and share everything like a real family.

They are my brothers, and though this is hard right now, I know how very lucky I am.

"You have a visitor, your majesty," the butler says with a bow.

"Very well. I'll be down in a minute."

"Not you, your majesty. Her Highness, Princess Lilya."

"A visitor for me?" Her nose scrunches. "Did Ronin turn around and come back here?"

The butler shakes his head. "No, your grace. A shifter woman. She's quite insistent."

"Fiora!" Lily squeaks, her smile lighting up the whole room. It's been so tense in here; the sight of something so bright fills me with fresh air. "I'll be right down. Thank you!"

She toes on her white silk house shoes while I bloom a lily from the center of my palm, plucking it and stopping her mad dash to the door. "Hold on. I want to make sure Fiora doesn't think you haven't been taken care of. She is your mother, after all. I'd like to make a good impression."

"You've already met her," she sniggers, stilling just long enough for me to pin the orange lily in her hair. A pink one would complement her lavender curls better, but the burst of orange feels more exuberant. More her.

"Yes, but this time I'm meeting her as your husband. It matters that she likes me."

She leans up on her toes to peck my lips. "Who wouldn't love you?"

It's a true testament that neither of us turns to check on Salem's state when she showers me with affection. We've come a long way in a day. We've got far to go, but our progress is reassuring, to say the least.

Salem straightens his military shirt and brushes his jeans as if that'll make them look finer. The moment Lily steps into the hallway, he's behind her, letting me take her arm but not allowing her out of his sight.

Des follows behind as we move down the steps to the receiving room toward the front of the palace and off to the side. It's smaller, for less important guests the fae royalty don't feel the need to impress. My father's a jackass.

"When it's my throne, we'll move Fiora into the palace so we can look after her."

Lily stops and turns to me. "Really? I mean, she probably will say no, but just you offering is... That means something." She taps her heart. "Thank you."

"Of course. She's your mother. I would say let's move her in now, but I'm not sure she'll be comfortable with my parents. I can't always intercept Father's snide comments, and I wouldn't want to put her through that. But if you like, just say the words and I'll move her in today. She can stay right down the hall from us."

She looks up at me like I'm the first man to pay her any kindness, which I know isn't true. Even though the three of us go out of our way to spoil her regularly, we're new introductions to her life. "You love me. That's love."

"Fiora can have a room in our mansion," Salem volunteers.

Des nods. "Our castle as well."

Though it's clear Lily wants to see Fiora right this second, she takes the time to kiss each of our cheeks. "Thank you," she whispers. "I love you so much."

Though her love is directed at all three of us, it doesn't feel less, like I'm only granted one-third of her affection. She wholly adores all three of us.

When we approach the receiving room, Father exits with his nose wrinkled. "That woman is insufferable. She claims to know how to defeat the Gorgonell, but won't elaborate on a single detail. As if we haven't exhausted every avenue." When my eyebrows shoot toward the ceiling, he holds up his hands. "Have your conversations, then get that shifter out of here. One in our palace is more than enough." He looks Salem up and down with a shiver of disgust, though Salem's made it a point to start bathing daily while he's got access to unlimited water, so he smells nice for Lily.

I stiffen. A slight on shifters is something I can't keep

quiet about anymore. "Enough, Father. Fiora can stay as long as she likes. I'm sure you have far more important things to do, like slapping the wrists of gruesome criminals."

Father excuses himself with a grumble, unable to part from the controversy fast enough.

The moment we enter, Lily runs to Fiora, throwing her arms around the old woman's neck and helping her to sit in the nearest chair. The housekeeper will have a fit about the dirty cloak touching the upholstered chair. Of course, that thought only drives me to set a footstool beneath Fiora's feet, smirking that it'll be dirtied as well. "Nice to see you, Fiora."

"Now, now. I hear you're to call me Mammy. Since I crossed into fae territory, it's all anyone's talking about. Ye married my bonnie lass, who's already wed to the vampire prince. Well done, tricky fae." She leans forward and grants me a toothless smile, pinching my cheek with filthy fingers. "Every now and then, the world needs to be turned on its head to shake out the useless junk. I trust you're handling the chaos with a steadiness tha gives my Lily reassurance you're worthy of her?"

I nod once. "I'm trying." And I truly have been. Twice a day, I sneak out to get updates on the tenor of the people, and see what fires I'll need to put out once Lily's more settled. There's much to be done, and I'm supposed to be on my honeymoon.

How am I supposed to enjoy my new bride with my

two best friends hanging around and a territory on the verge of a huge change?

Her wrinkled mouth pulls to the side, her head tilting with compassion. "You're worried. More than worried. You're drowning."

Damn that she can read me so well. "You think a fae prince will drown after a few licks? I'm sturdier than that."

Her eyeless gaze holds mine, spearing through my stiff upper lip faster than the most skilled interrogator. I've barely been in the room a minute, and this woman already spots all my insecurities. I can't take care of Lily well enough. The General's not in prison. Every day, the grumbling against the throne and against my wife grows.

I step back and Fiora takes her time turning her chin in each of our directions, her sightless gaze lingering longest on Lily. "You're fae," she remarks. "Do ye look the part now?"

"White dress. White shoes. Ivorum hair clip."

"Tha's as it should be."

Lily lowers her chin. "I can't tell if that's a good thing or a bad one."

I stiffen, hating every moment Lily's forced to question her heritage, the great blood she's part of.

Fiora chortles, easing my frustration. "It's only a good thing if ye make it so. Magic is what ye make of it. My child, don't ye know tha the fae need ye?"

Lily bands her arms around her middle. "I'm not sure they're super happy about uniting themselves with the vampires."

Fiora tsks her. "I'm not talking about tha. Unity is a dream tha will take years to come about. I'm talking about the need they have now. The miserable fate only ye can save them from. I heard much about it on the journey here. It's why I've come."

Lily's eyebrow raises, and for the life of me, I'm not sure what Fiora's getting at. "The fae have lots of challenges, Fiora. Which one is Lily suited for solving?"

She clucks her tongue at me. "Ye can call me your mammy now, not Fiora."

The word has never tasted sweet on my tongue, but I give it a try anyway and see how it fits. "Very well, Mother." Yeah, still weird. "We're not in the habit of putting Lily in more danger, so what do you suggest?"

Her voice is grandmotherly and comes with a warble, which I find endearing. "How many citizens has the Gorgonell turned to stone?"

My spine straightens. "I believe the count is at two-hundred-twelve. None in the past few months. We've moved everyone who lived in the area to new land closer to Neutral Territory. It's not ideal, but no further encounters with the Gorgonell have happened."

"The creature comes out at dusk, aye?" Fiora rests her cane across her lap before unfolding her plan. "Then my vampire son won't be part of this journey." She holds up her hand at Des' protest. "Lily's work must be done in the daylight, as the Gorgonell comes out at dusk. I do not wish to put her life in jeopardy."

"What work?" Lily asks, arms akimbo. "Of course I

want to help the fae, but I have no idea how to turn someone back to life when they're frozen to stone. That's what it does, right?"

I nod. "The Stone Graveyard is where the Gorgonell lives. It's a massive bull that's fueled by magic gone wrong. It was meant to be a weapon we could use remotely, so we wouldn't have to send our troops into battle, but we were never able to control it. So the beast turned on us, freezing innocents to stone whenever they looked into its eyes." I'm ashamed at the hubris of my people, but I make an effort not to brush our crimes under the rug. "We put up an iron gate to keep it hemmed in, but a lot of damage was already done. We can't destroy it. We can't save the fae who've already been turned to stone. The most we can do is contain the damage."

Fiora reaches for Lily, holding tight to her daughter's hand, though she addresses me. "Contain it and pretend it doesn't exist? I think tha line of thinking should end with your da. Ye are my good lad, are ye not?"

"I'm certainly trying to be. I admit, I do not know how to defeat the Gorgonell, and I love Lily too much to let her near the creature."

Her wrinkles gather at the corners of her mouth when she smiles. "Ah, but tha's what Lilya was built for. Best not rob the world of her magic. It's simple, really."

Lily drops Fiora's hand and crosses her arms over her chest. Her hip cocks to the side, and I can see the outline of her dagger, holstered beneath her dress. "Care to explain?"

"Aye. It's no more complicated than drawing out someone's disease or poison and taking it into your body. Then your system rids the world of the curse, as it's meant to do."

Lily's eyes dart around, like she's worried we'll learn one of her secrets, but we already know she can do that. That's how she healed Ronin when Prince Harris was poisoning him.

I chew on the inside of my cheek. "I mean, I didn't guess her gift could be multi-purposed like this. But the magic that's turned the civilians into stone is technically a curse. She can really draw that out?"

"It's going to hurt her," Salem protests. "When she took Ronin's poison from him, her hair turned black and she was out of it for like, a day or two. If she takes the curse from the stone figures, will tha turn her to stone?"

Fiora fiddles with the edge of her knitted blue shawl. "King Ronin had months of poison built up in his system. His daily doses received for months took her only tha small window of time to expunge. The stone curse isn't something tha keeps growing. It's a one-time blast tha has a lasting effect. Her muscles might stiffen after a while, but she experiences a poison or a disease's effect at a fraction of the potency the sufferer does. Then it's gone. Perhaps she can't heal all two-hundred-twelve fae in a day before she feels stiffness in her bones, but she can do much more than ye think." She beams in Lily's direction. "Though, tha's always been true about my wee lass."

Lily's voice is steady, her mouth flattening in a tight

line. "If I turn to stone after healing people for a while, then what?"

"I imagine it will wear off, just as every disease, curse and poison has worn off once your body figures out how to attack it. If ye feel your joints starting to stiffen, give your body time to clear out the defects. It always does." Her mouth curves up at the corners, as if this conversation is the time for delight. "Perhaps ye haven't found your place here yet, but I can see it clearly. The fae need to be set free from the evils they've created. Ye, my lass, have come into their lives for such a time as this."

Lily bows her head, her hands clasping under her chin. When she finally speaks, my heart sinks. "Okay. I'll do it."

"Of course ye will. You've never been content to let anyone suffer without just cause."

Salem's chin moves from left to right over and over. "No. We'll move the stone statues out of the area, and then she can try." He shudders. "Come to think of it, no. If you're wrong and she turns to stone after healing them, there might not be any coming back from tha. It's too much guesswork. Too many assumptions tha life will all work out just fine because ye have a good feeling it probably will. No. She's my mate, and I say no. I'm not letting her run headfirst off a cliff this steep."

Fiora's eyes widen. "What did ye say? She's your…" Her head whips from Salem to Lily, so Des gives the succinct explanation of the phenomenon none of us thought possible.

"Curious. Very curious indeed. Do ye have physical proof?"

Salem stares up at the ceiling, his arms crossed over his chest. "One of my eyes is fae blue, and the other turned from light gray to dark, like a mated shifter."

"Clouds! Are ye telling me the truth, lad?"

"Aye. I wouldn't dare lie to Lily's mammy."

Fiora lowers her chin. "Lilya, how will this work?"

She addresses Lily only, and it's clear she doesn't want us to reassure her we won't let things get out of hand. They've already spun too far out of our control as it is.

Lily wraps her hand around Salem's forearm and Des', and then connects her glance with mine to unite the four of us. "We're working on it. I'm married to Des and Lexi, and I'm mated to Salem. We didn't plan for that last part to happen, but it's not exactly something that can be undone."

"Indeed. Are ye prepared to spend your life with these lads? Because while marriages can be dissolved through much turmoil, mating is permanent."

A flicker of worry slices through Lily's confidence, but her chin raises after a beat of pause. "I'm certain this is what I want. They're good men."

Fiora smacks her lips for too long, calculating... I'm not sure what. She doesn't say a word as she drums her fingers along the top of her thigh, her chin lingering in Salem's direction as if she holds him most responsible. "Very well, lass. If this is your path, then ye must free your husband's people. They've been captive too long, and their own king's been powerless to save them. Go."

Lily nods, and I can see the resolve that won't be undone, no matter how many arguments we conjure up.

Salem doesn't like being overruled. None of us is thrilled with the idea of possibly putting her in danger. But he falls in line with Lily's decision, clearing his throat before turning away. "I'll go pack our bags for the trek." Then he pauses, as if his feet won't let him leave unless he's certain Lily's alright. "Ye got her, Des? Alex?"

I take the empty spot on Lily's side. "Of course, brother. If we only have the daylight to work, we should go as soon as we can."

Though Lily converses easily with Fiora about our exchange of vows done in secret, her hand trembles on my arm. I run my tongue along my top row of teeth, wondering just how dangerous it is, this good we're about to do that could go so very bad.

19

THE STONE GRAVEYARD

LILYA

I'm nervous, my stomach in a tight knot as Lexi shouts over his shoulder that the iron fence has come into view. I need to get better at riding. Carriages take too long for travel when we've got limited hours to accomplish all that needs to be done. Riding on horseback is the smartest thing to do, but I'm unpracticed, so I've spent the whole two-hour-long ride worried I'm about to bounce off the back end.

In case it's been undersold, let it be known that horses are tall.

My fingernails dig into Salem's taut abdomen, but he hasn't complained once. I don't like that the four of us have split up, but there's no getting around daylight, and none of us are willing to risk Des' safety in a carriage all day long when we don't know how dangerous this is going to turn out to be.

When our horse slows to a trot, Salem rubs his massive

palm across the backs of my hands. "Easy, Mate. We're here." His words come out sweet and gentle, but his body is tight and on high alert. "I've heard of the Stone Graveyard, but I've not seen it since the first wave of fae were turned. There are so many."

Lexi hops off his horse, guiding it by the reins as he walks over to us, reaching up his arms to help me down. "Two-hundred-twelve affected fae is just a number. Until you see it all, it doesn't feel real. I've got a few friends in here, and none of them deserved this."

A gasp fills my lungs at the sight I'm unprepared for, though I've known this was what we were coming to see. It's different up close. We slow to a trot as we near the formidable-looking iron fence, which stretches two stories into the air, warning every fae that danger lurks inside. There are massive rings of barbed wire strung across the top, making it impossible for the beast to escape. The space between each iron post isn't more than four inches. "People can still make eye contact with the monster through the gaps in the posts. Why aren't they closer together?" I wonder aloud.

No one answers me, which is a worry. Did no one think of that? Or did they just not care enough to do the job correctly? I can't decide which one is worse.

A distance beyond the fence is a stretch of house-lined land with stone statues. It looks like it was a neighborhood, once upon a better time, and now it's remnants of something that used to be. Something that should be, and possibly still could be.

Lexi leads us to the gate and unlocks it with a key from his belt. With how little resistance Lexi received when he mentioned he was going to show me the Stone Graveyard, I think his father was more than happy to get rid of us for the day.

One step inside feels like I'm walking on hallowed ground. The air is still, our bodies disturbing a silence not even the birds will break. There are no songs here. It's not even midday, but the sun looks dreary, almost perplexed that it should shine here, on the terrified faces of men, women and children who are frozen in various stages of panic and pleading.

Tears well in my eyes. Though I haven't felt aligned with my fae heritage in so very long, I am part of these people. Their pain is mine. Their fear rises and screams, even though their mouths make no sound. They were silenced because a few madmen thought they could win wars without getting their hands dirty. They wanted control, not peace. And now they have neither.

Salem's hand on my back is reassuring. That happens every time I get worked up about anything. He gives me a steadying touch to remind me that we're connected, that life's nightmares won't be endured alone.

"Take a minute to soak it all in," Lexi encourages us, his voice quiet as he moves into the immobile throng with purpose. He's looking at the faces, cataloging which ones he knows and which he does not. He pauses near one that's positioned away from the others, studying the face with a firmness to his jaw.

There's a statue of a mother throwing herself in front of two petrified children. I don't know why that one hits me hardest, but as stalwart and on-the-job as I was set out to be today, emotion wells in my throat and threatens to spill down my cheeks if I don't get myself under control.

So I look away from the mother. I glance away from the children. I turn away from their pain because part of me is a coward who can't look directly on life's atrocities. I'm ashamed of myself, that I can't even angle my body towards her agony.

Something firms up in my chest. Whatever reluctance I entertained about this plan, it's gone now. That woman deserves to see her children. She's earned the right with her mama bear heroics to have many memories with them, untainted by the terror of losing all that's precious to her.

Fiora was right to send us here.

"So many," Salem murmurs to himself. It's then I spot the same softness in his eyes that I'm trying to wall myself off from. Salem is stronger than me in this moment because he looks at the mother and the children, sharing in their torment when I'm too afraid to examine life's horrors up close.

I borrow a portion of Salem's fortitude and finally face the woman and her children. Her mouth is twisted with fear and pain, which is to be expected, but there's a noble lift to her chin that tells me she knew the stakes and made this choice anyway. She understood she would be sacrificed if she went out to rescue her children from the beast. She protected her family as best she could, and even though some might say she failed, a sense of triumph rises in me. There are good people in the world, even when it seems like there's corruption everywhere you turn.

I need to apologize to her for turning away.

She will be the first person we try to cure.

Maybe I'm supposed to wait, but my feet move forward with purpose. Her slender fae figure is dressed in a knee-length gown, frozen mid-sway. She's got her hair pinned in ringlets around her face, her lips pursed against her fear. Against the monster. Against fate. "I think you've been tortured long enough," I tell her, studying the lines of her face before I reach over and hold her hand, which is outstretched to shield her children from the monster who left her long ago. She shields one boy and one girl, who can't be more than three and five years old respectively.

I glance toward houses inside the walled-off area, and I wonder if one of them is hers, or if she happened to be out for a stroll at the wrong place and the wrong time, back before the iron gates were constructed. Giant cobwebs over the doorways are a testament that all things beautiful and strong will fade and be forgotten.

I need to learn this woman's name. I need her not to be forgotten. Does she have more family? Friends who mourned her absence? Does the world feel a void now that she's silent? When she could speak, what healing did she bring to her corner of the world?

What healing have *I* brought to my world? Fiora had to put the puzzle pieces together for me to even realize I could be an asset in this crisis. I'm ashamed it didn't dawn on me that I could be useful, that even cast-outs like me have a purpose.

I'm not sure what I expect to happen, but Salem yells for me to stand back. "Be careful, Lily! Ye can't just go touching them. We need a plan or something."

I shrug, holding onto the stone because I don't have it in me to abandon this woman. "I *am* the plan. I think they've waited long enough."

Lexi trots back to us, watching the exchange warily. "You have to do the chant, Salem. The shifter chant Fiora taught you to draw out the poison."

I wish I could do this without Salem, so he could be shielded from all of this, but it seems we were destined to be a team.

Salem begins the charm only a shifter can perform, which comes out in a series of syllables I've known forever, but can never remember on my own. Without a shifter to perform the charm to draw out the curse, my twisted magic is only good for creating poisons and death. Without my deranged magic, the shifter charm to draw out a curse or poison is useless, since it spreads the second it hits the air, unless I'm there to capture it and take it inside myself. My body understands what to do with all the bad things of the world. Destiny is forcing fae and shifter to work together, our sides marrying so we can liberate those on the brink of being forgotten. That nature or the universe or whoever will go to such lengths to get enemy sides to come together like this gives me hope that the four of us are on the right track.

What we want for the world might just be what the world desires for itself.

The entire charm takes a few minutes to deliver, and halfway through, Salem gets frustrated with himself and pulls out a sheet of parchment Fiora scribbled the entire thing down on, just in case. Gotta love her.

Lexi watches with such intensity, my palms begin to sweat. He knows this woman, perhaps, or is haunted by the fact that he doesn't. With hundreds of thousands of fae in Faveda, he can't be expected to know them all by name. Yet he studies each statue with a grief that looks personal, piercing sharply his most tender spots.

No more. The moment Salem cracks out the last syllable, I hold tight to the woman's hand, willing her poison, curse or disease—whatever this is—to leak out of her and flood into me. It will be a lesser version of her malady, but I know it will hurt. It always does.

But I feel nothing. No sensation at all. "Are you sure you read it right?" I ask Salem.

Salem turns the paper over. "Aye. I mean, I've never done this before. I have no idea what I'm doing, since we aren't exactly allowed to practice a charm this dangerous in school. But I did as Fiora instructed. What happens next?"

"I'm not sure. It usually just…" A trickling sensation tickles my palm, stilling my movements. "There it goes. It's happening."

At first, it's a tinkling of a leak, the curse dripping into my skin at a leisurely pace. When I inhale, the floodgates open, and I'm inundated with more than I'm prepared for. It's usually a steady stream of sensation, but this is like getting struck over and over. I hold on tight, trying to keep my calm through it. I'm sucking every bit of the curse from the woman, whose fingers grow warm in my grip. Her scream that started however long ago finally completes itself, belting from her lips as color washes over her from head to toe. The gray surface is replaced with life, the likes of which frighten me through my excitement.

Pink. Her pinned ringlets are light pink.

"I'm sorry," I whisper as she breathes her first breath in far too long. I should've been here sooner. She's been screaming for who knows how long, maybe years, but I never took the time to hear her until now.

"The Gorgonell! He's going to..." The woman looks around, staring at me in confusion as she drops my hand. The second the contact is broken, my whole body feels the weight of the curse. It's like sand is filling my limbs, stealing my energy and making each movement too much an effort.

My knees buckle and Salem drops his parchment, catching me before I collapse on the ground. He lowers me gently, and I don't fault myself for letting his strong arms cradle me in the grass. "Easy, pup. What do ye need? How can I help?"

"My babies! No!" the woman shouts, her agony ripping my chest open at the rawness of her love for her family.

"We'll free them. I know it's all very frightening right now, but we won't let them stay like that. Give it a few minutes, and we'll bring your children back." Lexi leaps into the role of consoling the woman who's too frightened and turned around to be reasoned with right away.

Luckily, whether or not he knows who she is, she recognizes him. "Prince Alexavier! You must run! The Gorgonell will come for you!"

Lexi has his hands full, but he turns her from the ghastly sight no mother should have to see. Then he sets about explaining all that's happened to her, and how she's come to be awakened.

"It's not the eight hundredth year of the sun. It's seven-hundred-ninety-nine!"

Lexi's got his work cut out for him, but I'm too weighted to be of any use. My chest is heavy, and each breath is a struggle. Though, as the seconds tick by with Salem fretting and driving himself insane trying to speed my healing process along, it doesn't take more than a minute for the pressure to begin to lift. I can breathe easier, and my heavy limbs are lighter once more.

"Fiora was right," I tell Salem, who's rubbing my arms with a manic look widening his eyes. "It was a curse, not a poison. I'm only taking a portion of the impact, and then it's leaving me." I lift my hand up and curl my fingers, testing how easily they bend. "Salem, we did it!"

Salem's not convinced until I'm back on my feet again. He puts me through a round of light calisthenics more to calm himself down than anything else. When I move to touch the little statue boy atop his head, Salem stiffens. "What do ye think you're doing?"

"Two-hundred-eleven to go. Come on. Start up the chant."

Salem shakes his head. "I can't watch ye almost faint again! We got lucky once, but what if it builds in ye? What if there's some cumulative effect tha's still coming? We've done enough for the day. Your hair turned black, ye know. Granted, it was only for a minute, but tha scared me!"

"No!" the woman screams as she drops to her knees, her desperation thickening my resolve that this boy must be healed next. "Please don't leave my babies like this!"

Lexi has his hand on the woman's pink ringlets, with her on her knees before him. "More, Salem. If we go at this quickly, we can liberate a third of them before the sun sets."

"A third?!"

I blink up at my fierce protector. "I love that you love me. I love that you want me to stay safe. But this is about more than just me. I'm their princess, Salem. If I could help them but I choose not to because it's a little inconvenient, then what good am I?"

Salem rips the parchment from his back pocket, glaring at Lexi and shooting me looks that communicate his very real worry for my well-being. "This is madness. But if ye need it, then this is what you'll have, for however long I can stand it."

Lexi helps the woman to her feet, his arm bracing her as she wobbles from too much emotion of learning that more than a year of her life has been erased. They watch without speaking. The only background noise to Salem's chant is her occasional sob.

The boy finds his way to his mother's arms.

Then the little girl, but I can't stop there.

A farmer, brought to life.

A father, and then his child.

A seamstress.

A blacksmith.

I need to go faster. I need to help them all.

20

FADING SUNLIGHT

LILYA

"This one next," Lexi urges after corralling the liberated toward the gate. They stand on the other side, too afraid to be near the beast's cave, which is still farther away than I could run to without getting winded. They wrap their fingers around the wide iron posts, watching and weeping as we move toward the statue Lexi selects. "I need to start taking groups of them to safety. There's a village not too far from here. If I can walk them there and borrow a carriage or something, Trey here can help drive it back and forth." He lightly claps the man's stone shoulder. "I graduated with him. We had a few classes together and always got along well. He needs to be next."

I nod and wait for the minute-and-a-half charm to spill from Salem's lips. I don't want to admit that my chest feels tighter than it should. I only hope Salem hasn't noticed that my recovery time increases by half a minute after each healing.

When Trey comes to life, his wide nose and broad mouth finishing the cry he started years ago. Lexi waits until Trey's blue eyes fall on his, and then grabs him up in a hug. "Trey, you're safe. The Gorgonell won't come near you ever again."

Only that's not true. We're merely bringing people back to life. We are doing nothing to stop the actual source of the problem. These iron fences won't hold the monster forever. But I let them have the lie because, like the others, Trey is turned around and grief-stricken over the lost time.

That, and my jaw has gone slack. Salem's good at catching me before I fall, for which I'm grateful. But the fact of the matter is, my body is working overtime to expunge this curse from the land. My heart is racing, my breath comes in shallow pants, and everything about me feels too heavy for proper use.

Salem's worried, which isn't anything new, but instead of fretting and rubbing my muscles, he kneels down, gets in my face and studies the pain I won't speak aloud. My lips remain shut but my eyes are screaming.

Salem's mouth is pressed in a firm line of displeasure. "This is too many people too fast. We're taking an extra minute or two between healings from now on. Ye won't do anyone a lick of good if ye die." He says it flippantly, but his throat chokes out the last word. "Ye don't have to move this fast."

"I don't want to stop," I argue the moment I can access

my jaw. I belong here—maybe not in Faveda, but in this graveyard, this forgotten space. I was built for times like this. I've finally found my place among my people, and I don't want to lose my hold on finally feeling connected to my kin. "They need me."

"Tha'll always be true. You're new to being royal. The people will always need saving. The land will always experience some irreparable distress. Problems will always arise that demand your attention now. But one thing matters most, so bury it in your heart." He thumbs my chin. "Ye cannot help anyone if you're dead. Killing yourself for a cause only hurts the world. So take the breaks ye need and make sure ye have the strength to stand before ye force yourself to get up."

Salem is wise, and I love him for it.

He glances at the nearest screaming stone figure. "These statues have been here a long time. If they have to wait another day or two, so be it."

I want to thumb the sharp edge of his cheekbone, but my fingers are still weighted. "If I had to be parted from you for a day or two, I'm not sure I could stand it at this point."

Salem looks shocked that I echo his attachment. He's been the one hovering, making sure we're not parted. But the truth is that I love it because it means he's near. Perhaps I'm not supposed to feel the mate bond because I'm not a shifter, but it's there all the same, tugging at my bones and course-correcting my heart so we don't stray too far from each other. All my stormy chaos quiets when he's near.

"Ye feel it too?"

I manage a nod, for which I'm proud of myself. Any movement at all is a victory as my limbs slowly begin coming back to themselves. "I don't want us parted," I rule. "And there are people in here that have been separated from their loved ones long enough. They shouldn't have to wait another day or two."

I had only Fiora most of my life. Now I feel connected to too many people. Married and mated. But this new tie on my heart is too much. This connection I feel to the fae is tugging at my spine, jerking me to act instead of wait.

"They're afraid, Salem. I'm linked to them, so I can't stop until every last one of them can choose their home. None of them chose this."

I didn't get to choose my home. They should have that power.

Salem doesn't argue further with me, but after each healing, he makes sure I've had some water, that I can do a few pushups, and insists we wait until I'm not wobbling on my feet. The one time I did, he made me lie down in the middle of the field for twenty minutes. I could've healed four people. So I take it slower now, my bones aching as the sun hangs low in the sky.

"That's enough for tonight," Lexi calls across the way to us. "We need to head on home. The Gorgonell comes out at night, you remember. Let's get the rest of these fine fae to the village, where they can regroup indoors."

We're further in the thick of the statues now, farther from the gate than we meant to go. "Seventy-one," I manage to work out from my supine position on the grass. Parts of me are numb, and the other parts hurt, but I manage what I hope is an unaffected expression. "Seventy-one healed, lots more to go."

"A third of them healed," Salem agreed. "Tha's seventy-one more than anyone's been able to help. Well done, pup."

I love his body, but I can't feel it. I can sort of move my limbs. Almost. But I have no sensation. My arm is pressed against his stomach as he holds my hand to his heart, but I can't feel him. "Salem?" I whisper, listening to the weeping of the dozen or so people who are making their way toward the gate. "I can't feel you."

Salem hoists me higher and rubs his bristly cheek against mine. "Do ye feel tha?"

"I do."

"I'll never leave ye, Lily. Even if ye can't feel me, I'm always here. Take your time. Just relax. We'll be back at the palace soon enough."

The air has been filled with crying and questions for so long that the sound of angry shouts breaks through the stone graveyard like the crack of a whip. "No! Let us out!"

It's the only thing that could part Salem from my side, but he only makes it five steps before returning and lifting me up. "I know this hurts ye, pup, but I can't leave ye out in the open like this. Let's go."

My teeth grind as my bones wobble in ways they're not

supposed to. Any movement is painful as sensation finally begins trickling back into my body.

"No!" Salem shouts, his boots pounding toward the fence. "Open the gate!"

I can only just barely see who Salem is yelling at. A few steps more and I can make out his stalwart expression. Everything in me tightens and threatens to run, if only I could access my legs.

Salem's feet slow as he reaches the gate with my head lolling over his forearm. "It's nearly dusk. Ye know ye can't lock us in here!"

My heart thuds in my chest when I turn my head just enough to see the terror.

The iron gate that's been open for the victims to go free is now shut, and by the looks of the panic striking everyone as they throw their body's weight against it, the thing must be locked, too.

When I was a little girl, there were high expectations put on my education. It wasn't enough to pass my tests, which was a struggle for me; I had to get the best grade. I rarely got more than half credit, since I could only complete the written exams, and not the practical ones that pushed me to form plants I still can't make.

Instead of accepting the flunky I was, there were consequences. Since I couldn't do a lick of magic, the General decided to motivate me with nontraditional methods. Oh, how I longed to please him. I would have done anything to make him proud, but I simply couldn't.

Milly was a nice girl. Quiet and kept mostly to herself

on the playground. She was just plain better at cardinal charms than I was, so she earned the most impressive grade in the class. Everyone else finished well above me, leaving me dead last.

The night after he learned I failed yet another big exam, my dinner was given to the dogs. I was reacquainted with the switch that cracked across my little trembling hands. Worst of all, I was locked in the study, where I wasn't let out until the next morning for school. I'm sure other children have it worse, but for me, being locked in any room by myself was frightening. I cried for hours, sobbed at the door as I begged the General to let me out. But he didn't budge. And in the morning, it was not him who liberated me, but our cook, who promptly quit later that day.

Staring at the General's firm glare now through the few inches of space between the iron posts, I know that no matter how hard we beg, that gate will not open. He will do as he does, because that's the power the world has granted him.

I guess King Fairbucks didn't lock the General up for more than a day, if he followed through on his word at all. I scold myself for being shocked that bad men do bad things.

Lexi gasps, and my eyes follow the direction of his and land on a body strewn in a bloody mess a few yards behind the General. "Is that… Did you murder Trey? Did you kill the man we just brought back to life?"

The General laughs. "Your go-between? Indeed, I did. No one is coming back for you now. The liberated will go on to seek out new lives, and no one will think to check back here for days. You know how self-absorbed our people can be."

"Your daughter is in here, you monster!" Lexi cries, thinking of me when his own neck is also on the line.

"Then it seems I've solved two of your father's problems in one go, and rid the world of a filthy shifter as a bonus. Did you really think old Fairbucks would lock me up for good? Shame on you for being so stupid as to think I'll ever get more than a slap on the wrist. I'm too valuable to the throne. Much more than you." He snarls at my husband, and it's then I see that the General is all alone. There are no soldiers who would go along with this, and that small concession gives me hope. "King Fairbucks' insipid reign will end by morning when his son is found turned to stone. Then the fae will see a new family put on the throne. One that doesn't allow our people to be polluted by lesser beings. You are reckless, Alexavier, but your father is foolish to have let you get away with this much hoodwinking. You've always been a slippery one, and I've decided the people won't suffer through another minute of your silly ideals. I've seen enough of your future. And it seems you have, too."

Salem's arms are vibrating with rage. "Unlock the gate!"

General Klein snickers at Salem, which is just about the most obnoxious thing he could do. "Without you to look after your people, they'll soon die off. When they do, their wasteland will be ours. Oh, the things we could do with Jacoba. A well in every city I think is a good start."

I don't say a word to my father's taunting because I know it will do no good.

Then General Klein summons up the nerve to grin and wink. "Enjoy your last sunset, kids."

Salem sets me on the grass and throws his body against the gate. It's a testament to the fine fae craftsmanship that it doesn't bend or bow under his massive girth. The wire overtop is barbed and far too dangerous to try climbing.

The General ignores Salem's attempts at escape and crouches down near where I'm lying. He cannot reach me, not even with a sword, but Lexi draws his knife just in case, and moves to stand near my feet. I don't know what he could possibly say to me after everything that's happened.

When his wicked eyes twinkle with triumph, I know my father will always be the man who loathes me most. His words come out slow and soft, like he's saying something sweet. "After all these years, you are still my biggest problem."

My heart thunders as devastation, fury and madness combine until something precious breaks inside of me. The fae woman who guarded her children from the beast gave her life for them. My father will stop at nothing to take my life from me.

Then my father walks away, his white uniform spotless in the fading sunlight.

21

SACRIFICE

ALEXAVIER

"We cannot get over it, Salem!" I shout at my deranged friend.

"I can climb anything!" he roars in my face after falling for the fifth time.

"Alright, if you can, good for you, but Lily can't. The others can't. I can't. This thing was designed for the Gorgonell not to be able to climb out and spread its plague to the rest of the territory. We need a different plan."

Lily can't lift her head yet, which is no small worry. When we first started, she didn't need more than a minute or two to recover, but this is going on ten minutes, and she's utterly limp still. I'm kneeling by her side, gripping her hand, but there's no indication she can feel me.

If I'm worried, there's a whole other word for what Salem is. He's on the border of unhinged as he slides back down the mere ten inches of purchase he gained. He's panicking, which sets my mind into planning mode.

My key was in Trey's pocket, for him to let himself in and out when he took the next carriage full of fae to the safety of the nearest village.

I can hear the snort of the bull in the distance, his grunts coming from the cave. I've never seen the Gorgonell, of course, only drawings of what some of the fence's builders saw of the sleeping beast when they were installing the barrier. A bull. A massive bull who turns people to stone with a single glance.

We can do this. *Come on, Alex. Think!*

"We don't have much more than a few minutes of daylight!" One of the liberated shouts. "You've set us free only to let us be captured again!"

Well, how do you like that?

I shove down my attitude and lift Lily up in my arms, seeking what shelter we can find. We only need to make it through the night. Then we can… I don't have an answer to what happens next, but now that the field has more room to run, I can see my options a little clearer in the dying sunlight. "The houses!" I call to the others. "Let's find a house we can wait out the night inside."

Though their muscles haven't been used in too many months, they dash full-force toward the few houses in the distance. We're half a mile away from shelter, but it's our only hope, so we make the most of the few minutes we have left. Even Salem abandons the hope that we can make it over the fence tonight, and turns to run with us.

I'm sweating, not just from the exertion of running while carrying a full-grown woman in my arms; it's anxiety that chokes me around the throat. "Salem, Brother, you have to take her. If the bull catches me, it doesn't matter. You and Lily have to make it to the house together. You're the people who can bring us all back if we're turned to stone!"

Lily lets out a bleat of fear that tugs at my heart, but Salem sees my point and slows for the tradeoff. I draw my knife to protect them as best I know how, running alongside them to block view of my family with my body.

My family.

Salem's always been my brother, but now I have a wife. I have a wife who can't lift her head. I have a wife who could be turned to stone in a matter of minutes because her father is a murderous villain.

And also because I allowed this entire venture. I secured the horses and brought us to this awful place. If she turns to stone, I will be the man who led her here. This whole thing is my fault. She was living a normal-ish life in Neutral Territory before I convinced her to marry Des.

If anything happens to Lily on my watch, Des is going to throttle me.

The sound of the bull's call across the field sounds like he's taunting us, telling us he knows we're here. It's been a while since he's had fresh playthings. Our fences have worked in keeping him sequestered from the rest of the populace.

"Eyes on the houses!" Salem calls out to the others, warning them that the goal is nearing. All we have to do is be faster than the Gorgonell. Faster than a charging bull.

The sun vanishes, and my heart sinks. I hate the words that spill from my lips, but I've never had such clarity. This is the choice. This is the way I can protect my family. "If we cannot make it, I'll draw the bull away. Get her into the house and stay there until morning."

"No!" Lily screams.

She loves me. I can hear it in her heartbreak. I try to force nonchalance into my tone, which is a true feat while I'm running with all my might and, you know, terrified. "You and Salem can free me in the morning. Promise me you won't come out until dawn."

"I promise, Brother," Salem replies, and I can tell he's working to the same conclusion I landed on—that Lily and he are irreplaceable on this mission, but I am not. I am expendable, and I'm okay with that.

Hooves hit the ground with a heavy pounding that makes my chest vibrate. I'm tempted to look to the left to view the massive girth that must be this elusive Gorgonell, but the goal is still to outrun the beast, not draw a true-to-life rendering.

The two in the lead splinter off, each checking a different house to play our odds at finding an open home we can hide inside. I cry out when I see both front doors fling open, relieved that my people will be safe.

The hooves are too close now. A statue hits the ground too near us. Without looking, I know we will not make it. Salem can only run so fast with Lily in his arms.

I swallow hard. "I love you," I tell them both. It's a

promise that I will return, a sad reminder that I must vanish for a time if they are to live.

"Lexi, no!" Lily sobs in time with Salem letting out an agonized cry.

The sound of my wife's anguish has an odd effect on me, simultaneously breaking me and rallying my last vestiges of strength. A burst of energy shoots through my body as I turn, keeping my gaze downward so I can see the beast's meaty legs. They're brown and dripping with a wet, black oil-like substance.

I do what I can to draw his attention from the others, who are reaching safety one person at a time.

This is what I want. This is the plan. He's turning towards me and leaving the others, giving them the time to find their shelter.

As I run, I reach down and touch the ground, sprouting a tree that grows slower than I would like. My hope is to trip the Gorgonell up, even to set up small obstacles that might make him lose momentum. Though, each attempt slows me by a second or two, which is time I don't have to spare.

My arms pump as I race through the night, dodging between stone statues. I make a wide circle and try to make my way back toward the houses. I'm so very far now, but I give it all I've got.

Lily's in the house. Salem's in the house. He's standing in the doorway with his back to us, listening without being tempted to look accidentally.

Though my footsteps swallow the divide between me

and my family, I know I cannot outrun a charging bull. I can either be gored to death or turned to stone.

"Barricade the door and close the shades!" I call to Salem, taking my last few steps before angling my chin over my shoulder.

The air stills in my lungs as gray eyes bigger than my fist bore into mine. I want to cry out, but my mouth won't move. My legs fill quickly with the heaviest molten rock, slowing my steps until all I can do is wobble to the side so the Gorgonell doesn't pierce me with his three-foot-long horns.

I stumble and fall, my arm outstretched toward the night sky. Lily calls my name in the dark, but I cannot answer her.

I cannot move.

22

LILY'S MAGIC

SALEM

My muscles are locked down as my back rests against the bookshelf. I've barricaded all possible points of entry, but the Gorgonell keeps trying to push his way in. He's too wide for the doorway, but all he needs to do is gain an opening to get his eyes on us. The bed frame has been turned on its end and pressed to the window. The bedroom has been shut tight. We're all huddled in the main room, listening to the sounds of sobbing and the occasional scream when the Gorgonell throws its weight against the walls. Even during the periods of silence, they're all huddled against the far wall tha has no windows or doors. I'm a dirty, violent shifter, and they've been taught not to get near me. Normally tha stuff doesn't bother me. I'm not overly fond of fae anyway. But being tha I just helped free them, I'm more than a little disappointed they can't see past our differences, even in a crisis like this.

Lily has no qualms being near me. In fact, her rail-thin body burrowing into my side is just about the only thing keeping me sane. Alex is out there, a sacrificial stone statue so we could escape. I hate tha I left him, but I still can't find a way around the logic. I'm a shifter, so only I can perform the charm tha draws out a poison. Lily's the only one who can rid the world of a person's curse. It seems fate was trying to keep the solution to so many problems away from us by keeping our races divided.

Now we have a chance.

One of us is rocking back and forth, but I can't tell which. I experience my woman's panic as sharply as I feel my own.

Grain. There's a tin of grain in the cupboard, along with a bottle of olive oil. No water, but one of them can use their magic to conjure some water from their hands. They can sprout plants to eat. We won't starve if it takes us longer than a few days to make it out of this place.

"Come over here," one of the fae shout-whispers to Lily. "Let her go," he commands me in what I'm sure is supposed to be a voice of authority, the pipsqueak. Alex trains with me every now and then, so he's got more muscle than your average waif of a fae. This lad's probably my age, and off his nutter if he thinks he's going to tell me what to do.

Then it dawns on me. "Ye think I captured Lily. Ye think I'm going to hurt her."

"Let her go, and I won't think that," the man replies.

Fair point, but still no. I'm not capable of releasing her.

If the Gorgonell bursts into the house, I'll be able to shield her with my body.

Lily's voice sounds exactly like a lass who's trying to keep her cool through being abducted. My woman's terrified, and this moron is making her uncomfortable. "This is Prince Salem of Jacoba. He's my boyfriend."

At this new label, my chest expands with permanence tha feels almost painful, like my body can barely contain the joy it feels at being linked with her in her language. For me, it's mating. For her, we're dating. I love it.

The concept is so strange to all five of them who are huddled in the far corner tha they cease all whimpering to gawk at us. Let them stare. Let them see how she glues herself to my body when she's scared. Let them wish they understood what we have.

"You passed out back there, bringing us back to life. You must've hit your head. Come here, girl," the man beckons. "What's your name?"

I'm confused when she stands, her legs unsteady. I'm worried tha she might actually go to them to appease their prejudices. Her fists are shaking at her sides, and I know this is the last thing she wants to deal with right now, what with Alex frozen outside. "The world is changing. You've been gone for quite some time, so be patient with yourselves when you integrate back into a society that doesn't hold the same prejudices you were raised revering."

Jays, she's perfect. Even though I know she's trembling on the inside, her words come out clear and focused.

Lily's eyes are filled with compassion. "Not everything

is as it should be, but not everything is as it was. The territories are starting down the road to uniting."

"Uniting?" A shriek tumbles from the gob of one of the lasses. "What are you talking about? Uniting with shifters?"

"So far, we have a peace treaty with Drexdenberg, but yes, Jacoba is next. This is a good thing, no matter how it sounds."

I listen to her explain with passion to rival the most enthusiastic saleswoman all the ways tha unity will benefit all three territories. She tells them of her marriage to Des, which is so shocking to them, they don't jerk at all when the Gorgonell pummels the side of the house. She's unapologetic about her marriage to Alex, and assures them tha all four of us couldn't be happier tha she and I are mated.

Mated. Never thought I'd see the day.

When she finishes her speech, they are not convinced, but they don't question her either. She's spoken with such authority and kindness tha I can't imagine how idiotic a person would have to be to try to tear apart her logic.

When she makes for the bedroom, I stiffen. "Stay in here, Lily. I can't be sure everything's boarded up properly in there. Some of the windows were only blocked with sheets and stacked boxes."

"I'll be quick," she promises. "And I'll keep my eyes on the floor, just in case."

I can't. It's sweet tha she believes in me enough to think I can let her move closer to danger without me there to shield her, but I don't have it in me. I stand through my exhaustion and go with her into the bedroom. "What do ye need in here?"

She keeps her word, and her eyes survey only the floor. "Just… Ah. There we go." She lifts up some linens from the floor and tucks them under her arm.

We go back into the main room, which is a better choice, with bigger pieces of furniture to block the entry points. She hands out blankets, because my woman thinks about other people. "I know we're not going to get a whole lot of sleep tonight, but it's drafty, so at the very least, we can get comfortable while we wait."

The others start trading stories about who they were before they were frozen, and what they were doing tha led them so close to the cave. I couldn't care less.

When Lily sets a flat pillow on the ground beside me, I raise an eyebrow. "You're tired," she explains. "You need to lie down, and I don't want your head on the bare floor."

Her words seem simple enough to outsiders, but to me, they're precious. Everyone assumes shifters don't need or want things like pillows and blankets, because we can sleep on the floor out in the open easier than the other races. The fact tha she treats me like a man with dignity gives me just one more reason to love her. And really, tha list has been piling up for five years.

I lay in front of the barricaded door and pull her down beside me. "If we survive the night, we're still stuck in here," she whispers, keeping her worry from the others while they talk about the lives they've been missing out on. "We can't get out."

I hold her in my arms, unsure if it's wiser to guard her from the Gorgonell or from the fae in the room. I settle for blocking the doorway with my body, and wrapping an arm around her to shield her from the whispering fae as best I can. "Des will come for us," I promise her. "They can provide food and water to sustain us. All we have to do is keep reinforcing the houses while we wait for help to come."

"I can't do magic," she explains while she squirms, reminding me of her limitations. "So I'm useless for growing food or conjuring up water."

"Now, what do ye call sucking the curses out of all these people? You're a lot of things, pup, but none of them are useless."

She smells like lilies, peaches and soap when she burrows into my chest. "But I don't actually do anything for that. I'm just a vessel. You did the charm itself. I'm sorry I can't make food or water like the rest of the fae."

I kiss her forehead. "Then they'll repay us for their freedom by keeping us alive. See? Nothing to worry about."

As if on cue, the house shakes with a jolt from the Gorgonell throwing its massive body into the side near the bedroom. The whole structure groans, and though it's been doing tha all night, this assault seems particularly brutal.

A splintering sound accompanies the next crash, and when I look up, one of the beams near the bedroom has cracked. Sawdust trickles to the floor, and I know it'll be a miracle if we last until morning. I'm careful as I sit up, pulling Lily with me. "Over to the far wall," I instruct quietly as I stand. There's a series of chairs and a table bracing the window opposite the front door. My movements are graceful and soundless as I make my way to the door, motioning for one of the lads to follow me. "We need this table to hide under if the roof collapses. When these beams start to come down, it's not going to be pretty, aye?"

To his credit, he doesn't shudder away from me, but nods through his fear. "How can I help?"

Good. He's got some sense. "I need ye to make sure the towel tha's over the window doesn't fall down. Can ye hold it in place while I move the table?"

"Sure, man. Of course." He gets into position and nods, the barely-there red scruff on his chin making me guess his age to be around seventeen or so. "Alright, I've got it. Go ahead."

A fae and a shifter working together without a fight. It's nice, despite what we're up against.

Once I've got the table away from the window, one of the lasses darts across the room and touches a board on the wall a few times, plopping something into her palm, then handing it to the lad.

Tacks. They're tacking the towel in place, which makes me want to kick myself for not thinking of it first.

Another crash against the frame, and I motion for everyone to huddle under the table. They almost fit, with the exception of one brave-faced Lily, who is biting her nails. She's been holding back to keep herself controlled, but something in her seems on the verge of snapping.

"Under the table, pup," I instruct her. "I don't want anything falling on your noggin."

She shakes her head. "There isn't enough room. If you turn into a wolf, you'll fit."

I scoff at her protest. "You're smaller than my wolf. Under the table, Lily."

Instead of listening to me, she stands. "I need to do something, but first you have to turn into your wolf and get under the table."

I rear back, shocked tha she thinks I'm capable of taking shelter for myself over keeping her from harm. "Do what ye need to from under this table. Now, Lily!" I don't think I have it in me to raise my voice at her, but I'm as close to tha as I'll dare.

Everyone under the table screams when the house endures another attack.

Though the fae are tear-streaked and cowering, her voice is calm. "We don't have much time. I can end this, but I have to go into the bedroom alone. We both know this house isn't going to last the night. It might not last another five minutes. Stay here. I'll be right back."

My upper lip curls. "Not on your life. We stay together. No way are ye going into tha bedroom! Tha's where the Gorgonell is aiming, smashing himself into tha wall."

"Then I have to hurry! I can get us out of this, but you have to trust me."

I don't trust tha she won't sacrifice herself for these quivering fae who've never deserved her. "If ye have a plan, then I'll go with ye. Either we live together or we die together. I don't much care which at this point, so long as we're together."

She acts like my words stun her, like she's taken aback by my unswerving devotion. She looks truly terrified, though her fears don't seem to be directed at the bull or me as she clutches the fabric of my shirt. "Please let me go alone. You won't love me anymore if we go together. Please, Salem. Let me be selfish. Let me keep you. Believe me, that won't happen if you come with me."

She's afraid I'll leave her? Tha's mad.

"I've never heard you say anything so ridiculous in all the time I've known ye. I'll risk it, whatever it is. You'll get under the table after we do whatever ye need to do in the bedroom?"

She nods somberly, like she's resigned to me walking out on her or some nonsense. She's already darting around me, aiming her steps toward danger for reasons I can't begin to understand. She has to throw her weight against the door to open it now, and I know it's because the structural integrity of the house has been compromised.

I curse loudly when I see the wall dented inward, too many beams splintered inward from the impact of the bull's girth. "Hurry, Lily!"

She shuts the door behind me, and there's a control that trumps her trepidation. It's hard to look away. "Cover your nose and mouth. Take a big breath and don't inhale until you're in the main room with the others. Understand?"

"What?"

"You cannot breathe in here, Salem!"

"Why?"

She's wringing her hands with regret and anxiety. "Because I'm about to fill this place with poison! Promise me you won't take a breath."

"What are ye talking about? What poison? Did I miss something stashed in the closet?"

She doesn't answer, but waits for me to comply. I feel stupid when I make a show of drawing in a long breath. I quickly cover my nose and mouth with both my shirt and my forearm.

I don't understand what I'm looking at. I mean, Lily can't perform magic. She's told us as much loads of times. Calls herself stupid, which guts me. But I can't blink through the sight of her blooming purple flowers from her palms. Most fae sprout one plant at a time from their palm, but the petals are shooting out from her like confetti. This isn't a fluke, some burst of magic she's unprepared for.

She knew she could do this.

"Don't breathe!" She reminds me through her tears. "They're poisonous. One plant can make a full-grown man lose consciousness for a day at a time, and I'm growing a lot more than a single plant here. I can't take any chances with a creature this big. The stench will build up. When he breaks the wall and gets inside, this should be enough to take him down at first whiff."

She's breathing the poisonous air but isn't fatigued by it. The moment the petals pile up along the battered wall and make a two-foot wide line, she spins on her heel and grabs me by the elbow. She jerks me into the main room and runs for the far wall, snatching up a sheet. She crams it under the door, making sure no polluted air reaches us. "You have to shift, Salem. If you breathe in too many toxins, you could pass out, or worse. Just to be safe."

I stand gaping at her, wishing I had the time to do things like demand some sort of explanation, but it's then tha the house gives a deafening groan. I shift into my wolf and dart to her, snagging my teeth in her pant leg and directing her to the table. She doesn't put up a fight this time, but crouches under the wooden shelter as the bedroom begins to splinter apart.

I don't understand what I saw, or maybe I do understand, but I can't fathom it. All I know for sure is tha my mate is terrified, so I move around to shield any exposed spots with my body while the ceiling begins to fall around us.

23

A GIRL BORN WRONG

LILYA

The silence is scarier than the sound of wood breaking. The deafening nothing has been ringing in my ears for two minutes now. "Everyone, stay where you are." I should keep the bite out of my voice, but I want them to be afraid enough to fall in line without a fight. Here only Salem knows my horrible secret, and he barely understands the tip of the madness. If word spreads about what a horrible person I am, well, there goes any chance at uniting the territories.

I crawl out from under the table, feeling like I'm walking through a haze, as if my body isn't attached to me. It's walking toward the bedroom, but am I? Normal movements are too surreal for my mind to latch onto. I'm horrified, terrified, not just of the Gorgonell waiting for me, but of the fact that another person knows my secret. My father and Fiora are the only ones who knew, and now Salem.

Best case scenario, Salem will leave me for all I've done.

Worst case scenario, Salem will have no choice but to tell the others, who will have me put away. I deserve to be punished for capital crimes I committed when I was a girl.

I didn't mean to kill my classmates. But this is different. Now murdering with my dastardly talent is intentional. I need to take down this Gorgonell. I need to free Lexi, even if he leaves me after Salem tells him all I've done.

Instead of opening the bedroom door, I opt for moving the furniture blocking the front entrance, in case any toxins waft through the air towards the cowering fae. I don't know what Salem's take on any of this is, but he skitters out from under the table and trots by my side until I pause, my fist on the handle. "You can't follow me, Salem. I can't have you breathing in anything dangerous. I'll go check."

He whines and flattens his body to the floor. I know he doesn't like staying behind, but he understands that this next part is above his pay grade. My footsteps are careful as I move out into the stillness of the night. It seems even the leaves are afraid to rustle. My feet are silent as I walk on the grass, my heart pounding with every step I take away from the severely compromised shelter. My eyes are on the ground, in case the Gorgonell ran off and might be somewhere in the dark, looking for me and biding his time until I glance up.

I'm cautious as I round the corner, my heart in my throat and my stomach twisting with too much trepidation. I feel every switch of the breeze, every thin hair on my arm that rustles. I'm on high alert until my eyes sweep over the bull's hoof, splayed and motionless as it rests partway on the grass and part on the floor of the bedroom, atop bits of the splintered wall he managed to collapse. My gaze climbs up the rest of its body, stopping at its brown, furry neck which is thicker around than Salem's shoulders. The beast is enormous, and whatever relief I feel that it's been subdued is swallowed up by a sick wave that forces my lunch to rise in my throat. There is no way any team of soldiers could have taken this mammoth creature down. Those poor fae didn't have a chance, and are lucky they were turned to stone instead of trampled, or gored by its javelin-like horns.

No one is watching me, so when my knees buckle by its side, I don't feel ashamed. His ribs are moving slowly up and down. Though he's sleeping now, I know that won't be the case forever. The purple petals haven't blown away because the wind isn't all that bold in a place like this. The wind knows better than to make its mark on this forsaken part of the world.

I move around the bull toward its backside and get on my knees, digging in the dirt with my fingernails to make a hole deep enough to bury my crime. Over and over I claw at the earth, hoping to dig a pit big enough to hold all my indiscretions. This spot in the earth will bear the worst of me, keeping my shameful secret so the world can find a way to smile at my face, as if nothing at all has ever been wrong.

Nothing will grow in this spot ever again. I swallow hard as I scoop the petals into the hole that can never be deep or wide enough to hold all my many sins. I don't often think of myself as fae, but I feel it in my bones as guilt swarms when I purposely murder a portion of the ground. The poison is too strong for anything to bloom here ever again. I leave a trail of death in my path whenever I trick myself into thinking I can be me—that the world has a place for a girl born wrong.

I scoop the dirt and grass over the petals, and already, the grass begins to wither.

I'm a murderer.

So I know the next step to take.

I dig deep in my reserves, fishing around for the correct mindset to produce what I need to finish the job. It can't be a run-of-the-mill poison for a big guy like this. It has to be planned to scale. I remember watching fae teachers grunt with the effort of producing the bits of nature they needed. Some are easier to bring into the world than others. Standard trees, though bigger, didn't look like they required much effort at all. Plants with purpose have to be finessed, and the one I need now is layered with purpose.

Finally, one small plant sprouts from my palm. It seems so innocent and sweet, this white flower. It doesn't look like much, but I remember Fiora training me how to weaponize this one. I don't know how she got her hands on a fae book of curses, but I've learned not to ask questions I don't want answered. She wore gloves, a mask over her face, and stood far enough away. Her distance made me nervous, her careful instructions of how the flower should be bloomed and administered set deep in my mind. Fiora was never afraid of me, which gave me license not to fear myself.

Though, in moments like this, I can't help the tremble in my lower lip. I barely remember being a little girl, but I know I didn't dream of moments where my purpose is to destroy.

My shoulders roll back as I give the plant its full minute to bloom and rest in my palm. Tonight, I remind myself, my mission isn't solely to destroy; I'm here to protect. I'm protecting my people, taking one step toward repaying Faveda for the lives I stole, back when I didn't know what I was doing. I'm protecting the fae prince, wicked as he might seem for scandalizing the nation with our funky marriage arrangement. I'm protecting Salem, who will most likely run from me the moment we're freed.

It's an effort to remind myself not to let my gaze slide over the enormous bull's eyes. I do my best to keep my focus on his jaw, parting his slack mouth and pressing the petals atop his wide tongue in a neat, slobber-stuck row. He stinks of rotting meat and mud, and I'm certain now I do, too.

When I close him up, I stand and jog back to the house, venturing in through the front door. Though no one in here is going to turn me to stone, I keep my eyes aimed at the floor.

Salem is still in his wolf form, which is probably best. We don't have to talk about any of it yet. I can pretend a little while longer that I'm normal, that he sees only my good parts.

"Let's go, guys. The Gorgonell is dead, but we should still get out of here. This house isn't exactly stable. Grab the linens and anything we might need."

Cries of relief are mingled with "how did you kill it?" I ignore everyone and trot to the second house, letting them know the good news. Their house isn't crushed to ruins, but the structure is on the brink of collapse on one severely bruised side.

Everyone has questions, stories and emotions bubbling out of them. I am so beyond all of it that everything pings off my chest. Nothing sinks in, only that I need Lexi. I need to see him look at me like I'm amazing, like I'm just the right thing in his life. I want to pretend, and I've learned fae princes can make you believe anything.

I stalk out into the night with my wolf mate by my side, in search of my fallen prince.

24

STOLEN BED

LILYA

"**S**alem, we need to bring the others back." I don't care if it takes all night. I don't care if I pass out. I want this done with.

Salem transforms onto two legs beside me. "Okay, but slower this time. More rest in between each one. You'll pass clean out if we rush it again."

Good. That's what I want. I want to feel nothing. To numb it all. If I have to poison myself to get there, so be it. I'm relieved Salem isn't asking me about it all, though I know it's coming.

I seek out Lexi first, probably because I'm selfish and need to see his face again. It takes some time, but when I find him, he's a tragically handsome statue with his belly on the grass, turning to look over his shoulder with determination slicing the terror in his eyes. He wanted to turn to stone, most likely to avoid being trampled and killed. He's always been the one with a plan.

I kneel beside him, my hand on his head brushing over his stone-gray motionless hair. Salem's eyes are on me even as he works his way through the lengthy charm. At the end, the trickle of numbness flows through my arm and sinks into my chest.

Ah, bliss. I'm numb and cold, heavy with physical weight that far out-measures the mental toll that living with my secrets has burdened me with. I fall back and stare up at the sky, letting the sound of Lexi fill my ears. He's coming out of his panic, but I can't help him. I'm not sure I have it in me to help anybody beyond sucking out their curses.

Eventually my body is cradled in Lexi's arms while he shudders, torn between overwhelming relief and fear of what's still lurking out there in the night.

"The Gorgonell is dead, but since we're still locked in here, we're not out of the woods yet," Salem explains. My gaze flits to him, curious why he didn't rat me out. Is he really capable of keeping my secret?

When my body comes back to itself, we move slowly through the statues, liberating and then resting for longer periods with little discussion in between from my end. Lexi and Salem talk over possible escape plans, but we decide to shelve any action until they're all awakened, which will take the rest of the night and all day.

Lexi enlists the help of two of the women who've had a few hours of adjusting to the transition to be able to lend a hand. Most fae are too shaken for reason when they come back to life, and it takes time to explain it all to them. So we liberate them, and then hand the new person off to the two women, who speak so gently to the newcomers, I often listen in on their kindness.

I blink up at the sky and let the women's assurances wash over me. "You are safe, fae child." "Come stretch your muscles and be at peace." They're so loving. I pretend they're talking to me. How my heart aches to be safe, to feel the freedom of being able to be me without breaking all that's good in the world.

There is much to do, so we work, with Salem repeating the charm over and over again as I take curse after curse into my body. We work through the night, through the day, and until dusk starts to set in. Lexi braces me so I don't clonk my head on anything when I go stiff. My limbs are so weighted and my brain too foggy for sense to slow me down until the last fae is finally liberated.

I'm so relieved, I want to cry, but I'm too tired to commit to the effort.

"Food," Salem suggests when my stomach growls. "We have to eat. Can ye ask your people to grow some fruit or something?"

"Fine idea, Brother. Look after Lily, will you? I'll get them going."

Salem doesn't sit by my side but lifts me in his arms. "I know ye don't want to be carried, but I can't stomach the sight of ye falling, so this is what it is."

Luckily I can blame my quietness on the physical toll too many healings is taking on my body. I don't mind him carrying me, actually. I worry this'll be the last time, though. He takes me into one of the unused houses, kicking the door shut behind him. After a quick glance around, he takes me into the bedroom, laying me down on someone else's dusty sheets.

I blink up at the ceiling, hoping he's not going to make me talk about anything. I'm exhausted, and ready to check out.

"So ye *can* do magic." Salem confronts me quietly, though he selected a house far enough away from the others that no one's going to hear our exchange.

Here it comes. I run my tongue across my top row of teeth before I speak. He hadn't said anything about it for so many hours; I was kind of hoping he'd forgotten. "Not like Lexi, no. My magic is different, and I try never to use it."

He sits on the edge of the bed, forcing a labored groan from the bedframe. He angles his chin toward me. "Ye told us ye were stupid, tha ye couldn't do magic."

"I am stupid. Children can sprout bushes. Teenagers can grow individual flowers and whatnot. I can't do any of that, unless it's harmful. I can only produce poisonous plants. No matter how hard I try to do it right, it always hurts people. So I pretend I can't do a lick of magic. It's safer for everyone that way."

Salem goes quiet for a few beats, so I stop breathing. I can feel our connection teetering on a precipice I've feared for so very long.

Finally his hand reaches over and rests atop mine, and I exhale. "Tha's not stupid. Tha's different."

I give a dismissive "pfft," but that's the most I'll engage.

He hasn't left me yet, so I take my good luck where I can find it and change the subject. "Why are we in here? The fae need us. They're all freaking out because we still haven't found a way out."

He kicks off his boots. "We're taking a break before we tackle tha. A nap. We haven't slept in a long time."

I would protest, but saying goodbye to the gloom of the night feels like the best option. Salem waits for my nod and then surprises me by taking the spot beside me on the mattress, folding the musty blanket over us. There are hardly any trappings in this room—a lamp, a bed, a chest in the corner and a fallen broom in another corner. Nothing important, and all of it forgotten.

I can't believe Salem wants to sleep beside me. I'm dangerous. "I won't hurt you," I promise. "I only killed the Gorgonell because he was going to collapse the house on our heads."

"I know." The corner of Salem's mouth draws upward, as if I've said something funny. "I don't think ye understand how deep the mate bond goes. Ye could stab a wee puppy kitten in front of me for no reason, and I'd figure out how to explain it away. Ye could stab me, and I'd be mad at myself for dirtying your knife."

My face pulls with horror. "Tell me you're joking."

"Your needs, and us being together, are the most important things. Everything else doesn't feel quite so urgent." He brings my hand to his lips and kisses my fingers one by one. "When ye wake up, there will be fruit for us to eat. We'll have a plan of how to get ourselves out of here. It'll all look shinier after a nap. The world always does."

He wraps an arm around me, and I'm unable to keep emotion from choking my response. "You love me." I have no idea how I got this lucky.

He brings his knee to sandwich between my thighs. "Aye. Always have."

To test his words, though I know I should take them as they come, I run my ringed hand over his chest. I need to hear the words, yes. To see the man beside me stay when it's impossibly difficult. I also need my ring to confirm Salem is the right man for me to gamble my future on.

"Oh!" It's a different sensation I get than when I touch Des' chest. With Des, I feel settled with this inarguable faith that he's not capable of lying to me. I don't get that same assurance with Lexi, but it's never bothered me. There's enough good stuff there for me to lean on. With Salem now, my hand heats up. Actual heat. It flows through my wrist like melting chocolate, relaxing my joints and reminding me that I am not alone. I live in Salem's chest, and he exists in mine. We feel like one body as my ring knits us together. Whatever lies he has, they are now mine, and mine are his. Though I don't know them all, they are my truths that I will swear by and take to my grave.

When my eyes meet the blue and gray of his, I know he's experiencing the same phenomenon I am. That though the world is broken, it breaks *around* us. It cannot break *us*.

"At last, ye got there." Relief coats his words as they kiss my face. Then his lips follow suit, meeting mine with acceptance of all the horrible things I am, and all the wonderful things I will never be. I'm his villainous queen, his wretched love.

His lips are velvet framed by soft pine, his prickly facial hair teasing and coaxing me to live the life I thought could never be mine. It was too grand to belong in my hands, yet here it is, begging me not to crush it. I've got Salem's hair tangled in my fingers as if some lost part of me deems it's finally safe to come home.

My leg has just enough mobility to wrap itself around his hip, marrying my pelvis to his. Salem's fingers dip inside the hem of my worn t-shirt, tracing lines on my skin that prove to us both that he's very much mine.

His tongue parts my lips, and I'm positive I'm levitating. We've transcended this house, this space, this world, and claimed our own. His shirt comes off because I want to admire the full expanse of him, memorizing his hairy chest with my hands and lips. I love the feel of him—so very male in all his parts. When my tongue sweeps over the low peak of his nipple, he throws his head back through a shiver that ripples through his body and jerks his groin closer. His hips grind into mine as he groans, hungry and determined, letting me know things are about to get real adult real fast.

My shirt slips over my head, and there I am, bared and open for him. My bra is lacy and white, which I was told is standard for fae women. It's definitely a step up from the ratty beige one I wore even after the underwire busted months ago. Judging by the widening of Salem's eyes, he likes what he sees. His large hand scoops my breast, thumbing the tip that can be clearly detected through the thin fabric. A soft noise of longing escapes his lips as my back arches into his touch.

He toys with me, taking his time to make sure he's lit each nerve ending on fire. I'm writhing in the sheets, gripping any part of him that hovers above me as he shifts his weight so he's caging me in. He's so very big, sheltering me with protection and affection while a wicked smile plays on his lips at making me squirm for him.

"I love seeing ye like this," he admits between kisses.

When the door opens, I freeze and Salem shields my body with his, protecting me even from errant glances.

"Might want to lock the door next time," Lexi suggests as his footsteps find us. Lexi's eyes climb up my body, his teeth digging into his lower lip. He makes his way over to us, nudging Salem aside. He leans down without hesitation to sweep my lips in a kiss that's entirely different from Salem's. His lips are soft but not as full. They're forceful and dominating, telling me what he wants. His knuckles graze down the scope of my bare side, forcing a rough cry from me as my hips jerk at the air, seeking out friction neither of them give me.

When the kiss ends and Lexi stands, pinching the bridge of his nose, I instantly crave more of him. "Man, this is just the worst timing, but Des is here. I came in to get you two."

Salem kisses my lips leisurely, as if the great news of our liberation is no big thing. "We'll be out in a minute."

Lexi sighs unhappily. "Might want to make sure it's only a minute. Des is in a right state, not being able to get to us."

We steal two minutes together, and then go meet Des at the gate.

ALMOST RESCUED

DESTINO

I reach through the bars of the gate, holding Lily's fingers. Instantly the void that's been growing ever since my family left is filled, the holes of my psyche spackled in with just enough hope to heal some of my more broken parts. "Blue eyes, are you well? You look like you haven't slept in a week."

She's got bags under her eyes and her fingers are stiff. Still, she does her best to reassure me. "I'm okay. We're stuck in here, though. Any chance you've got like, a key or something?"

"No key. Alex told me it was your father who locked you all in here?" I shake my head. "He's a right cruel bastard. I searched the dead bloke out here for the spare key, but General Klein must've taken it."

She leans her forehead on the bars that separate us. "We have to get out of here. I can't think of any way other than sending you back to the palace to tell King Fairbucks about it all. Then he can send you back here with a key."

My gaze flicks to Alex, and I hate that I have to tell him stuff like this. "King Fairbucks knows."

Alex grins. "Then we'll be feasting in no time. How far behind you is my father?"

I swallow hard, grateful the fae they've brought back to life are too afraid of Salem and me to get near enough to eavesdrop. I reach my fingers through the bars, waiting for Alex to take hold before I say the words I know will break him. Fae believe so strongly that the lies they tell are trivial, that they're justified, so the consequences won't be so bad. But when they're tricked by their own, the shock hits, contrasting the belief that people aren't completely dreadful. This time, they are. Or at least, their leader is.

I grip Alex's fingers, watching his free arm wrap around Lily, connecting the three of us while Salem flanks Lily's other side, his massive forearm leaning on the bars over my head. "I overheard General Klein tell your father he'd taken care of the problem, and the kingdom wouldn't have to be bothered by your interference with his plans anymore. The treaty with Drexdenberg is already in the process of being redacted. It's a mess. I stole a horse and rode through the night as soon as I heard." Serves them right for not remembering how hard it is for a vampire to sleep at night, especially on enemy soil.

Lily's gasp is a portion of the horror I felt when I first overheard the horrid plan.

I despise that I'm the one fracturing Alex's last shred of hope in his father. I can't even properly hold him while his worldview shatters. Now I've got two fae I love whose fathers care more about public appearance than they do about their own children. I trust Lily to hold Alex, and she does so without having to be asked. He's too stunned to speak, so none of us force words out of him.

I want to tell him it'll all be okay, but not once during my ride here did that feel true. It's going to be dreadful for a while, on both a personal and countrywide level.

Alex finally manages single syllables. "I... um... it's..." Then he closes his eyes and shakes his head, his next word coming out in a whisper. "No!" Then his eyes widen as they fix on a point over my shoulder, his whisper turning into a shout that blasts me in the face. "No! Des, run! He's got silver!"

I start to turn, but then a force I can't see slams my body into the bars of the iron gate, knocking the breath from me. I don't understand what's happened, and then something hot spreads agony through my entire being. My mouth opens, and I'm fairly certain sound comes out, but it's not making sense to my ears. This is different than the arrow piercing my shoulder. Something that feels like lightning and dread seeps into my veins. "Silver!" I manage, gripping the bars as my arms go numb on the outside, but turn to pure flame on the inside.

Lily screams and holds onto me, gripping my shirt through the bars, lowering me gently as I sink to my knees.

My legs are useless—numb on the outside while fire races through each artery. It's all I can feel, all I can think as Lily and Alex hold me tight to the bars, reaching around my back to rip the… knife? Arrow?

I don't feel my throat cry out, but I hear the sound of my shout as the sharp edge is yanked from the back of my shoulder.

The silver is gone, but it's too late.

Ronin trusted me to rule in his stead, and now I'm dying. I can feel the silver working its way into me, killing and deadening as it goes. I can't feel my hips, but for the fire that's erasing all other sensation.

Salem shouts at the offender, and I hear the General's voice saying… something as he approaches. He stands behind me and pats me on the head. Actually pats me on the head like I'm his dog. I'm dying playing the part of a fae's dog. I'm dying in front of my best friends who can't get me to safety. I'm dying in front of my wife, who stands and thrusts her arm through the bars, jerking her father by the shirt and banging his head against the iron. It doesn't knock him out, but the message is clear.

My wife will avenge me. She will find a way to tell the world I am no man's dog.

The silver must be warping my brain. A handful of purple petals fall like confetti all around me, and suddenly, I'm very sleepy. The inferno in my arteries dies down because, I realize, I am dying along with it. Pain means I'm alive, and now that it's going, so will I go into the void of night.

My body collapses, and the last thing I see is Lily holding her father's shirt to the gate while she stabs him in the belly with her silver dagger.

26

SILVER POISON

SALEM

There's so much blood; I don't know which puddle belongs to which body. Alex is in shock, but something clicks in my brain the moment Lily plunges her dagger into her da's stomach. "It's a poison!" I remind us all. "Silver is a deadly poison to vampires. If we can get it out, Des might live!"

"We just yanked it out, but it still stabbed him!"

I'm not saying it right, so I try again. "We've been purging curses all day and night. Maybe a vampire being poisoned by silver is no different. We have to try, Lily!"

Her mouth pops open as my words start to make just enough sense to her. Lily nods quickly, her dagger still in her tormentor's belly, the hilt still gripped in her fist. She looks like a wee girl, scared of standing up to her abusive parent.

But she did it.

I start the two-minute-long charm, frustrated with how

long the whole thing takes. I've never heard of a vampire living after silver made its way through their bloodstream. But this is the only hope I can grasp at. I need it. I need Des.

Des is my... I can't let this happen. I speed through the syllables, glancing at Lily, who yanks out her knife from her da's gut. She snatches the keys from the General's belt before she thrusts him backwards. He stumbles, but I know the wound isn't enough to take him out completely. She does her best to bend her arm around the bar to fit the thing into the lock. Her hands are shaking, but she finally turns the key, liberating us all.

But I don't feel free. Even as I run to the other side, working my way through the long chant, my chest is locked. I'm doomed to torment if the silver does what it's supposed to do to the friend who was never supposed to leave us this soon. I hoist up Des and run him away from the purple petals. I know they're powerful enough to knock out the likes of the Gorgonell, though she used significantly less this time.

I leave General Klein to bleed in the flowers.

T'was a thin silver blade I yanked from Des' shoulder, which I make sure is on the other side of the gate, nowhere near him. Though the puncture was small, the silver is determined Des will lose far too much blood. Silver wounds on a vampire always gush. My hands are slick as I turn Des onto his stomach on the grass, making sure Lily can get near the wound, if tha's a thing tha needs to happen.

The moment I finish the chant, Lily grips Des' shoulder, closing her eyes as tears rain down on his back. "It's not working!" she panics. "Come on, Des!"

Alex drops to his knees and flips Des onto his back, pressing down on Des' sternum in three bursts at a time, forcing his heart not to stop. "Breathe, Des! Just keep your heart beating!" Alex shouts, jerking my own heart around.

Des is too still between Alex's pumps. His eyes are open but they don't see me. They don't see my panic. They don't see tha I love him. The lads are always saying it to me, but I just grunt in response, as if tha's enough. "I love ye, Des," I tell him, though it's a pathetic offering now. "I'll take care of this. I'm not leaving ye here, aye?" I'm reasoning with a man who can't hear me. I scramble through the charm again, in case I missed a syllable in my haste. I'll say it a thousand times if it'll do a damned thing.

Lily's eyes are closed as she keeps her trembling hands on him while Alex pumps through intermittent shouts of terror.

Then finally, when I'm certain I will die right along with Des, Lily lets out a cry of relief. "I'm burning! It's working. It's working! It's okay, Des!" Her chin angles in my direction. "Des will be asleep for a while. I put him to sleep with the purple petals. I... Ah!" She screams, and I have half a mind to jerk her away from Des, but I force myself to let my mate burn from the inside out. My wolf howls, bangs against the cage of my chest to get to her, so I move to her side and brace her through the pain while it hits her in bursts.

The Gorgonell's curse was delivered in a blast, so it only takes her a minute or two to absorb those ones. King Ronin's poison was administered over the course of months, so tha took her a day or two to get out of her system. This silver knife was a burst tha didn't stay in Des more than half a minute, so I know my mate will only burn from the inside-out for no longer than a handful of heartbeats. Otherwise, I'm going to lose my mind. I'm on the brink as it is. My whole being is in agony, knowing she's in pain. A panicked whine escapes my lips.

Jays, I'm tired.

Not until she goes limp with relief do I realize Alex's eyes are starting to droop. "The purple petals!" she warns him in a quiet voice. "Get farther away from the flowers, or you'll all pass out. That's why Des is alive but asleep. We're not far enough from them. A few more feet should do it."

Alex stumbles away, but I can't separate my body from hers. I'm not capable. So I pick her up and move us both the requested few feet away, resting her back against my chest, which suddenly doesn't feel quite as tired. "So a few purple petals put people to sleep, and buckets of them can take the Gorgonell down?"

She nods, her eyes focused on the General, who's bleeding from his gut, surrounded by a small smattering of flowers. "Des will live. Des will live," she breathes over and over. "He'll get through this. He'll wake up. I can't believe that worked."

Alex is blinking at her from a few feet away. "What did

you do? You can't do what you did. You told us you couldn't. But I saw it. I saw you do magic."

I've been through the shock of this, but it's hitting Alex for the first time now. I'm just glad the other fae are far enough away tha they can't hear us.

Lily's breath comes slowly as she recovers from the trauma of taking Des' poison into her body. "I can't do normal magic, so what I told you was partly true. I can't even grow a tree."

Alex's eyes are so wide, he looks like he's seeing a ghost. He's frightened of this lie, of her. "Tell me the whole truth this time."

Her hand holds onto mine. She's scared. Maybe she's afraid to tell him. Maybe she's afraid of herself. I know she's worried she'll end up alone. Obviously tha's not going to happen.

"You don't need to know it all," she rules, not unkindly. I feel the tremble in her fingers, the catch in her breath.

"Tell me the truth!" Alex shouts, shifting from scared to livid.

Dread creeps up my spine when it dawns on me there might be far more to her story than even I know.

27

CRIME AND CONFESSION

LILYA

I don't know how to talk about it. The words have been stuck inside of me since I confessed my crimes to Fiora when I was eight years old. We don't speak of it. Whenever the panic bubbles up inside of me, I hear her calm voice. "Magic is what ye make of it." Then the anxiety settles back down.

But now I have to show my cards, tell the truth, and risk all that I hold dear. I need to hear Alex call me his Lily-girl again. I want him to look at me with that carefree "It doesn't matter that the world is falling apart all around us. I'm charming and handsome. Let's have a party," kind of way. There's a finesse to his relaxed hips, a sultry curve to his smile, and I'm terrified that once I tell him all he's demanding to know, those precious things will be gone from my life.

Alex points to the stretch of grass between us as the

breeze touches my hair. "You'll tell me everything right this second, or I swear, I will leave this place without you."

Salem stiffens behind me, his chest brushing my back. "Tha's a lousy bluff."

"I can't be married to someone who's got a whole bag of tricks up their sleeve! I can't be worried that at any moment, my wife's battering ram is going to take me by surprise." Lexi isn't blinking. "Talk!"

He's yelling at me, which isn't something I ever thought I would experience. Even when he got in trouble because I smeared blackberries on his white shirt when we were little, he didn't raise his voice at me. Maybe it was naïve to think we could continue on so simply. Maybe I should've told him the truth from the start.

Lexi loves me. He'll understand. I was wrong to have such little faith in the guys.

"It was an accident," I work out, my voice rough as the jagged confession forces its way out of me, slicing my tender spots just before it hits the air. I'm not good at talking about this, but I muscle through my resistance and assure myself that Lexi won't leave me. Salem didn't. Granted, he only knows half the story, but he didn't leave. I need to be brave. I need to be myself, even if that person has made some very bad mistakes. "When you knew me all those years ago, I was too young to practice charms and whatnot. You start that work when you're eight in school under lots of supervision. But I was ready. I had you, who was two years older than me and ahead in that respect. I read the entire textbook over the summer to prepare for being taught. I tried my best in school, but I couldn't make anything grow. Nothing at all."

Lexi glares at me. "Then you fake died. How much of your life is true? How many lies have you told me? Fake death, fake name when we met in the pub. Fake magical aptitude. What else?"

His words aren't uncalled for, but there's so much venom that I recoil. I hold tight to Salem's hand, knowing that if he keeps my grip, they won't leave the second they know the truth. I can't even feel relief that Des' chest is moving on its own, though he's still passed out.

I clear my throat, and though the rest of the rescued fae are out of earshot but in sight, it still feels like we're the only people in the world. My mouth is completely dry, but at last I untether myself from my worst secret, spilling it at the feet of the men I finally trust enough not to leave. "I practiced everything I learned in the textbooks, during and after school. I made sure to do it outside, so the General wouldn't catch me failing." I remember vaguely how elated I was that I could finally conjure up such pretty petals on my own. The burst of them blooming from my skin was something I'd tried so hard to achieve. "I made flowers just for me in the backyard. All different colors, and then crushed them so I could surprise the General when he got home from work. I didn't understand why the plants all around the crumbled bits immediately withered. I assumed I just was no good at magic yet, and needed the teacher to help me correct the mistakes I was making." Panic rises in my throat like vomit, trying to purge the poison of memory from my body. "I didn't mean to kill the dog!"

Lexi's eyes widen impossibly more. "Commander? That pit bull your dad loved?"

I nod, my stomach lurching as the name of the General's wrinkle-faced dog comes back from the recesses of my mind where I'd buried the crime. The memory of Commander sitting on my feet while I read in front of the fireplace hits me with such clarity that I can practically smell the stench of his fur after the rain. I think I suppressed a lot of my time with the dog we'd had since I was born.

I swallow the bile before it comes out of me. "He was digging in the flower bed, which always set the General off, but this time, he didn't come back inside with muddy paws. He didn't come back at all. I found him dead in the flower bed, near the flowers I'd torn to bits. That's when I first knew something was wrong with my magic."

I need Salem's steady heartbeat to keep me in the present, to keep me in one place. A vivid image of Commander with his four legs splayed in all directions, his caramel body motionless even after I picked him up. I cradled him like he was my baby, promising him all the ways I would make this better. I would wake him up somehow. Stop pretending to be dead. Doesn't he know how much that scares me?

"You killed Commander?" Lexi's face is gaunt.

I nod. "It was an accident. I didn't know the flowers I

was blooming were poisonous. I was trying for a small bush, like the book said."

Lexi's mouth is in a taut line, his disapproval firm. "You told me Commander got into something in the garden. You didn't tell me that *something* was from you!"

"I didn't mean to!" I plead, a tear running down my cheek.

Salem pulls my curls over his shoulder and runs his fingers through my hair. Salem isn't going anywhere. Lexi's mad, but he won't leave. I was eight years old. I loved Commander.

As if he knows what I need to hear, Salem says low in my ear, "Keep going. Get it all out. We're not going to take off on ye." He points to Des' steadily moving chest. I haven't even allowed myself to fully feel relief yet, so quickly did we dive into this mess. "Look at tha. Ye bring life. You're not a bad person."

I hiccup through the next bit, shifting my butt against the grass as I run my palm over the blades, leaning back against Salem. "We were supposed to try ferns in school later that week. Those are easiest, I guess. Everyone did their best. Some did it and some couldn't yet, but I did. Only my plant wasn't a fern, even though I followed the instructions exactly. My plant had little white petals. They were so pretty, I made more. Dozens more. It was easy. It was fun, even. I didn't connect the dots when everyone started choking except me. I didn't understand what was happening. Then the teacher grabbed her chest and..." The memory of the tall woman collapsing to her knees slams into me. "Then everyone got real sleepy. I wasn't sure what to do. I ran to my teacher and…" I remember poking at her, trying to shake her awake through my tears. "I was scared, being the only one alive, so I ran away. I ran home and hid under my bed. When the General found me, I told him what happened. He took me outside and told me to make the fern again. That's when we realized what had happened." I close my eyes through the memory of what followed. "He beat me something awful. Till he tired himself out. When he put me in the carriage, I thought he was taking me to jail for killing my classmates and my teacher. But he took me to shifter territory instead and dropped me off there, far enough away that I couldn't find my way home again. And well, you know the rest. I killed them." My voice feels loud, though it's barely a whisper. "I'm a murderer. My magic comes out as murder no matter what I do."

When neither man speaks, I confess my lesser crime, which is perhaps where I should've started. "My ugly cookies that I make to give people better dreams? They've got eevana leaves in them. In low doses, it takes away your nightmares. In higher concentrations, they can melt parts of your brain. I know how to measure the strength properly, but that's one of the other things I do with my magic I don't tell people about. It's not the extra sugar and butter that made them the top seller at the pub."

Lexi stares at me as if he doesn't know who I am, like I'm a different person on the other side of my magical malfeasance. Salem is still holding my hand, so I cling to the hope that somehow this will be okay.

"They don't punish children for capital crimes," I say once my tongue unsticks itself from the roof of my mouth. "But the General didn't want his name associated with someone who can only produce poisonous plants. When Fiora took me in, she wasn't scared of me. She brought me out into open fields and trained me how to grow different kinds of poisons. She taught me how not to be afraid of myself." I point to the purple petals surrounding my father. "Those put people to sleep. In larger doses, they can put a person in a coma. The breeze cuts the potency."

My gaze lands on my father, his belly bleeding as he moans through this haze. He looked so much bigger when I was young. Now he looks like an old, angry man.

I don't know how I find my way to my feet, but my wobbly knees manage to support me as I walk toward the General. I scoop up the petals and bury them, and then wait half a minute for the night air to clear the General's head enough for his eyes to open. Des is still asleep, but it's only a matter of time before he wakes.

I kneel beside my father, looking down at his salt and pepper beard that hides the scar he got on his chin from a run-in with a shifter battalion years ago. He blinks up at me with panic widening his eyes when he comes to. He knows it's time.

"I can't let you live," I tell him, afraid of him still, even though I'm the one in control this time. "You tried to kill me twice now. Tried to kill Des. Tried to kill Salem and

Lexi, too. Tried to kill all the fae you locked in the Stone Graveyard."

He murmurs something, but it makes no difference now. I lower my head and press my palms together, taking a deep breath to clear out the screaming in my mind so I can focus.

"No!" Salem shouts, jogging toward me. "No, Lily. This isn't the way."

I lift my head, tears streaming down my face and splashing onto my father. "You know he's a murderer! What I did was wrong, but it was an accident. He tried to kill Des on purpose!"

Salem kneels on my father's other side, his hand reaching across to still my wrists from their quaking. "But if ye do this, it will be on purpose. Ye didn't make tha choice when ye were eight, but ye can make this choice now. Let him be tried for his crimes."

I scoff. "We tried that already. King Fairbucks let him off without a blink for what he did to me."

Salem's eyes darken. "Let him be tried by Ronin for an attempt on the future King and Queen of Drexdenberg. Let him be tried by the Jacoba courts for trying to get me killed in this graveyard. I want him to live long enough to see ye inherit the fae throne and the throne of Drexdenberg. I want him to see ye marry a filthy shifter."

My heart stutters, but Salem doesn't give any notion that he regrets his roundabout hint at us getting married someday. "But he knows I'm dangerous!"

"And he won't have the audience to tell a soul. I'll see

he's buried so deep in our dungeons, he'll scream himself mute and no one will hear." He shakes his head at me. "Let me patch him up, and we'll take him to my courts. Ye cannot kill him, Lily. You're going to be a queen someday. This is the kind of skeleton tha doesn't stay buried." He motions to the fae in the distance who are watching without hearing. His thumb rubs slowly over the silk of my wrist. "Let me do this. Be the queen they deserve."

Too many things are rocketing around inside of me, but I know Salem is right. "He won't escape?"

Salem touches his heart. "I give my word. I won't take my eyes off of him until he's locked up." The moment I find the strength to nod, Salem calls over his shoulder, "Alex, help me with your new da-in-law. I need rope. A rope, a gag, and something to stop the bleeding."

Luckily, the General's lost too much blood to escape, lying pliant and weak as Salem gags my father before he works out two words. My mate nods in Des' direction. "Go sit with Des until he wakes, pup. Ye don't need to see this."

I take his advice because I'm just that overwhelmed, and the verge of shock. I don't know what the right thing to do is anymore.

PRINCE ALEXAVIER AND LILYA

LILYA

I'm surprised when I make my way over to my first husband and see Des' eyes are opened. I'm not sure how long he's been awake. "Did you…"

Des nods once, his gaze on the heavens. "I heard it all. Maybe I should care, but I don't. I'm alive. You saved my life. I felt myself dying. Felt my body burning from the inside-out." He glances down at his injured shoulder and frowns. "What happened to me?"

I scoop up his hand and hold it to my face. "Silver. The General got you with a silver dagger."

"No. I thought it was, but I'm still alive. That's not possible."

I do my best to give him a quick explanation of just how he escaped an early death. He's quiet through it all, but I can tell he's going to have questions aplenty. "You're really okay?"

Des angles his chin in my direction. "I'm not sure. I'm

too numb to tell. I'm alive, though. I think that's the important part."

My father's cry of pain sends a lance straight through my heart. I don't know what I want. For him to not be in pain? For him to be in lots of pain? For him to die? For him to be imprisoned? My fingers curl in my hair, gripping while I bite my lip through his scream of agony that I'm sure will never go away. That there are no good options feels like a condemnation I don't want to believe is possible.

"Don't look," Des instructs. "Easy, easy."

"I'm my father's daughter!" I whisper, though it feels like a scream. "I'm a murderer!"

Des' eyes don't condemn me as he keeps his spine pressed to the grass. He looks on me with compassion I don't have the grace to grant myself. "Come rest a while. It's been a long one, yeah?"

Des uses the hand I'm holding to pull me down to lie next to him. I curl into his uninjured side and let myself go, weeping into his cheek too many years of loneliness. "I'm sorry I didn't tell you sooner! You deserve to know who you're marrying, and I didn't tell you!"

Des turns his head so he can kiss my wet nose. "I married you the very first night we met. There wasn't much time for conversations and confession. I wager there'll be plenty more surprises ahead of us. I'm not mad. I get it."

A loud sob bursts from me as I drape my arm over his chest. "You're not leaving me?"

Of all things, Des chuckles. "Of course not. I've killed a few shifters, and it wasn't on accident. It was self-defense, granted, but I don't think any of us have clean hands at this point."

I kiss his cheek over and over, finding flashes of relief in the midst of my distress. Maybe the worst isn't going to happen. The thing I feared most doesn't seem to want to find me. Maybe life will give me a break after all.

Maybe I did find myself some very good men.

Lexi calls to the scared fae who've hung back. "It's time to move, people. There's a village nearby where we can get you some help. If any of you needs to come to the palace while you figure things out, our guest lodging is open to you. But first things first. The nearest village has agreed to take you all in and help you locate your loved ones. We'll march north. Are you all ready for that?"

They nod eagerly and file past us, most of them shuddering at the sight of a fae woman in a vampire's arms in the grass. I don't care what they think, and I'm not planning on moving from this spot any time soon. Des doesn't condemn me, though there are plenty of stones to throw. We do our best to ignore them while we cuddle in the grass together. He needs a little more recovery time before he can be expected to stand.

Des holds me with one arm as they file past us, his lips pressed to my forehead while Salem and Lexi finish bandaging and tying up my father. When it's time to get up and move, I see Salem's filled my father's mouth with his dirty sock, and then used his belt to trap it there. I don't know why I find that funny. As an inaudible snigger slips through my lips, I wonder if maybe I've hit some sort of tipping point with my sanity.

Des struggles to sit up, his eyebrows bunching together as he turns his chin toward his injured shoulder. "Odd. I can't feel my right arm. I can't move it from the shoulder down. That'll go away, yeah?"

I want to tell him something reassuring, but honestly, I have no idea. I don't think they'll tolerate lies at this point, even if they're the sweet sort of fibs. "I don't know. I've never healed a vampire from a silver infection before. I didn't even know it would work. Maybe you should see a healer, and they can tell you better."

Des nods, though I can see he's disconcerted as Lexi pulls him to his feet.

"I need a minute before we get going," Lexi tells us as the last of the fae pass us and start on their journey. He's not looking at me, which starts my stomach churning all over again. "General Klein is secured?"

Salem's eyes scan the abandoned field for signs of life. "Aye. Can they get to the village without us leading them?"

Lexi folds his hands over his chest like he's bracing himself from the weather, his shoulders hunched in and his legs shoulder-width apart, like he means business. "Yeah. One of the women is from that village, so she's going to lead the way." He still isn't looking at me. "This thing you can do, this secret poisoning ability you have?" He shakes his head. "I can't. Salem and Des didn't know you back then. It makes sense that you didn't tell them right away.

But you know me. And you had time to come clean. You should've told me before we got married."

My whole being stops all movement as the blood drains from my face. "You're right. I was scared you wouldn't want to be with me."

"Well, maybe I should've been able to make that choice. Now it's too late. I'm stuck in this marriage."

His words punch me in the gut. It's the thing I feared most, and it's crashing atop me in waves too terrible to seem real.

But it is real. Lexi won't even look at me.

He shakes his head, his eyes fixed on the space of grass between us. It's only a few feet, but it feels like a prairie of distance. "You trapped me. Waited until we were legally bound and then sprang this on me. What am I supposed to do now, Lilya? I can't exactly divorce you after making a big public spectacle of our relationship. And it's not just Faveda that's looking at our marriage. The whole of all three territories needs this to happen if we're ever going to unite. You trapped me!"

Lilya. He called me Lilya. He never calls me that. That's my name when I'm in trouble. I'm his Lily-girl. "I didn't mean to do that to you."

Des scoffs. "Are you having a laugh with this? Alex, you're being a prize idiot. She was eight years old."

Lexi points at me but still won't look in my direction. "But she's grown now, and should've told me I'm getting into bed with someone capable of murdering a roomful of children!"

He's not wrong, but his words have grown a fist and punched me in the sternum. I stumble back at the force of his fury. They're all true, these condemnations I put on myself. But hearing them come from his mouth, they sound cruel and unjust.

"Enough!" Salem's chest barrels as he moves to my side. He and Des flank me, but I don't want that. I want Lexi to be on this side too, not standing across from us with a tightness to his jaw that might never come undone. "She's not going around poisoning people now. I bet she hasn't done anything like tha since then."

"I poisoned the Gorgonell," I admit, though they already know as much. "And at the pub, I give patrons bits of a plant that makes them throw up when they've drunk too much and I'm worried they'll die. And I already confessed I use eevana in the ugly cookies. I do use my magic. But I don't go around killing people now."

"Now," Lexi scoffs. "Do you hear yourself? I was never the same after you died. None of those families who lost someone that day were the same. Don't you get that? You've gone from victim to murderer! I can't even look at you, I'm so mad."

"Prison," I suggest, my voice coming out hollow as my mouth goes dry. "I killed all those children. If it helps those families, I can go to jail."

"Stop it!" Des shouts. "This is enough. You're not going to jail for something you had no control over when you were a child!"

Lexi finally looks at me, but my whole body withers

under the hatred laced in his glare. Never has he ever looked at me that way before. "Convenient, you offering now. You know very well children aren't tried for capital crimes." He shakes his head at me, as if I planned this whole series of events. "And if you become a criminal in their eyes now, no way will they unify under your rule. I have no choice! We have to stay married and you have to keep your secret. Any window for confession to the nation closed the minute you stood to inherit the throne with me. They have to trust you if they're going to follow us toward unification." His accusation shoots out like a well-aimed arrow through my heart. "You planned this!"

This can't be happening. This can't be happening!

Salem snarls at Lexi, and I hate the sound. I don't want them fighting. "How? How was she supposed to confess to the crime when she was a wee lass? To whom? Her da? She did tha, ye pile of shite, and she was dropped off in Jacoba for it. She barely made it alive to Neutral Territory. She served her time, as far as I'm concerned. And don't forget tha we're the ones who came to her with our plan. This was *our* idea, and she went along with it. Don't let your gob run away with ye and rewrite the facts."

Lexi shakes his head, his gaze returning to the grass. "I can't do this. We'll stay married in name only. Everyone knows you're duty-bound to Drexdenberg and Jacoba as well, so it won't make them suspect we're through when you're gone. But you have to go, Lilya. I can't live with someone who would lie to me for that long."

My whole being crumples in on itself, and my knees go

out from under me. I drop to the grass, my face in my hands. Apologies spill from my lips, but I know there's nothing I can do. Lexi is through with me.

Alexavier. Prince Alexavier is through with me.

I don't see the punch, but the fist on flesh hits my ears and jerks my head up. "Salem, no! You love him!"

Salem shakes out his fist, his eyes murderous as Alexavier spits a mouthful of blood at the grass between us. "I love *ye*, Lily," Salem corrects me. "I know how you'll carry his blame around with ye. I know what it's going to do to ye, and so does Alex. He knows, and he's being like this anyway. Well, he can carry on by himself. Let the dead Gorgonell ye saved him from do all the listening."

"No!" My scream hurts my throat, but I can't be quiet about this. "Throwing me away is one thing. I deserve it, but you three can't throw each other away! You love him! You can't hurt him."

Salem grabs Alexavier by the collar and jerks him in the direction of the village. "Go be perfect elsewhere."

Des' eyes are wet, but he nods, confirming that Alexavier needs to leave. "Goodbye, brother."

I can't watch him go. I don't have it in me. He was taken from me when I was little, but now he's walking away on his own. He wants to leave me. I'm not his Lily-girl, and he is not my prince.

Salem kneels in my eyeline, lifting my chin with a touch so gentle, I never would've believed him capable of punching anyone. "He's having a bad day. Tha's all this is.

He'll come back when he's done licking his wounds. Until then, we're leaving this place."

Des winces as he helps me up with his left hand. His right arm and shoulder are still motionless. "I'm tired of the fae. We can go back to Drexdenberg or we can go to Jacoba. I don't care which. I need to find a healer, and I'm good to go wherever."

Salem nods as he watches Des fold me into his side. My husband's arm is around my back while I sob quietly into Des' collar. "Are ye sure ye don't need to be in Drexdenberg? You've been away for a while."

Des is resolute. "I'm not leaving my wife. Not after all she's been through. I'm not cruel enough to send her into Jacoba without me, where she was dumped and scarred when she was still a kid." His words are a dig at Alexavier, and even though Des didn't throw a punch, it's clear he's just as livid at the separation. Des kisses my forehead, and I swell with love for this great man I know I don't deserve. "It's going to be okay, blue eyes."

I'm shaking so badly; I don't know how my feet find their way forward. Des' arm doesn't move from around my back as we walk. Though he's the one who almost just died, he's more concerned with my internal injuries.

Salem hoists up the General, making sure to keep my father on a tether behind us, so I don't have to look at the man who hates me. Though General Klein is bound and gagged, I feel his presence. Each rustle of grass his boots make as they drag sets my nerves on edge.

"One foot in front of the other," Des says as he kisses

my temple. "Sometimes we don't know the whole journey, only one step at a time. See our feet?"

I glance down and notice that he's measured his longer strides to fit mine. "Yes."

"We'll get there together, yeah? Wherever we land, we'll get there together."

It's a small slice of solace, but I cling to the promise that the unknown won't always be this difficult. Des is with me, and so is Salem. And wherever they are in the world, Fiora and Ronin are in this with me, too. Though, Ronin doesn't know my secret, so I may only have this span of time before he finds out all I've done. Still, I'll take it. I'll scoop up the moments where I have four whole people in my life and hold them tight in my heart.

The journey to Jacoba is long, and will take many days, but the road ahead to uniting the territories is far longer.

"One step at a time," Des reminds me, his good arm bracing me and giving my side a squeeze.

So I take one weighted step toward the new way of the world.

Without Prince Alexavier.

Love the book? Leave a review!

Enjoy a free preview from Malicious Prince, and order the book today.

ONE.
Two Pinpricks

SALEM

TRAVELING like this is the worst. Forget the fact tha we've got the handicap of a vampire with us, who can only travel by night. Push aside tha Des is moving at half his normal speed, due to recovering from the immense blood loss from his silver injury. Forget tha we're traveling with the bound and conked out General Klein—a decorated and trusted arsehole who tried to kill Des, Alex, me, a whole slew of fae, and his own daughter. Ignore tha half of our party are not welcome in fae territory. It's the silence tha's killing me. All tha other stuff I could figure out, but Lily's lips haven't opened since Alex decided he couldn't live with her deadly abilities. I'm not sure if the tipping point for him was tha she kept it from us for so long, or if it's tha she can only produce plants tha harm or kill. Either way, I never thought I'd see Alex take himself out of the equation. Whenever Lily's around him, he brightens and softens and does all the things a lad in love does.

He'll come around.

"I can't," Des admits, holding up his left hand for us to stop. "I have to sit down."

"We've only been walking two hours. We have to make the most of the moonlight," I remind him. It's not like Des to ask for a break, so I know he's more injured than he's let on.

His breath comes out shallow, but his accent is perfectly proper, like always. "I lost too much blood. I'm not... I hate to be the one to bring up the fact that I'm a vampire, but, well, I'm a vampire, and I can't go this long fresh off an injury without blood to get me through. I don't know where to stop to refuel in this part of the world. I didn't pack extra blood because I was planning on us going back to the fae palace after I unlocked the gate to the Stone Graveyard and let you all out."

I tighten the reins of the horse I'm walking. The poor brown beast has the snoozing General Klein draped over its back. Lily bloomed a flower to keep him dozing, and tucked it in his lapel. "I can't even guess at where we might be able to get ye some filtered blood in fae territory."

Des swipes his left arm across his forehead to mop up the sweat. Faveda is tropical, but Des' perspiration doesn't look like it's from heat. He's fighting an infection. And losing. His right arm still hasn't been able to move, and it's been two days since we set off from the Stone Graveyard where we'd been trapped. We were trying to heal Faveda, and succeeded in ridding the land of the Gorgonell tha's been turning their people to stone. One would think tha would grant us a parade or at least a carriage to safe lodging, but tha's not how it's shaking out for us.

Good riddance.

Lily's been so silent tha her presence seems to fade into the background, though because we're mated, I'm still aware of every breath she takes. She's in agony, losing Alex to his anger, and there's no talking her out of punishing herself. She's not ready to speak yet, but she glides over to Des, who's given up on standing.

I have no idea what to do for him, other than keep him moving. "Let's go. The longer it takes for us to reach shelter, the worse this is going to get."

Des glowers up at me.

I'm not wrong. I mean, it's not like it's going to get easier for him to travel when there's even less blood in his belly eight hours from now. "I'm already at worse, Salem. Vampires can't live as long without blood as you all can go without food. And I'm coming off a silver injury, which no vampire's ever survived. I'm telling you, I'm desperate to drink, or I'm as good as dead out here."

I tilt my face skyward, asking the stars for any kind of guidance. Anything at all. "What do ye want me to do?"

Lily kneels in front of Des and tugs at her shirt collar, her eyes down and to the side as she offers him…

My stomach tightens in warning as Des' eyes soften. "I can't drink from you, blue eyes. The blood vampires drink has to be filtered. You know how it goes, yeah? Vampires drink filtered fae blood just fine, but not directly from the fae. In a pinch, I can drink directly from another vampire, but it looks like I'm the only one of me in fae territory." When Lily offers her neck again, Des places his hand on hers. "I'll only get sicker if I drink from someone who's got

Green Lightning in their system. All fae are guarded against direct vampire feedings when they take Green Lightning. It was a nice thought, though."

She shakes her head, tugging at her collar again in offering.

I don't like this. I really don't like this.

Des' eyebrows raise. "Are you telling me you don't have Green Lightning in you? You didn't get a booster at the palace?"

Another shake of her head. Another reminder tha I haven't heard my mate's voice in days. I'm on the edge of imbalanced with her locked in this depression. I don't have the cruelty to try to pull her out of it. Her life is pretty grim right now. To try and cheer her up would be insulting and ineffective. Her father tried to kill her—once when she was a wee lass, and again two days ago. Her fae husband left her in the same month they married. She's in a country tha's supposed to be her homeland, but not a stitch of grass anywhere is familiar to her. And I bet she's waiting on us to leave her next, which I've tried to assure her isn't going to happen. But I guess tha's not the kind of thing ye can tell a woman; she has to see it practiced—daily staying with her and reminding her I'm not going anywhere.

"No," I finally work out. My throat is parched, and I hope I'm hallucinating what I can't be seeing. "Ye can't let him drink from ye, pup." My attention switches to Des, who's sweat through his shirt and looks paler than a person has a right to be. "I would offer my blood, Brother, but everyone knows shifters can't sustain vampires."

Des' voice comes out cautious. "Lily, you should be on Green Lightning. That's so dangerous."

She shrugs. My mate shrugs tha she's not on the one thing tha keeps her from being attacked and exsanguinated by a vampire. Then again, maybe she missed her booster because we were expecting to go back to the palace, but ended up heading in the opposite direction. Still, my gut twists at the very illegal thing they should not be entertaining.

But Des won't make it to Jacoba without blood. My best mate will die if he doesn't feed soon. Everything in me is at war, so I stand stock-still with my fists clench. We all know this is the only option, and it might not even work. The blood's supposed to be filtered. But it's our only shot, so I chew on my lower lip and let Lily look after my best friend in the way only she can.

Des takes her hand with trepidation. "I've never fed directly from a person before. It's not exactly something vampires are allowed to do. We don't even have the opportunity, as you're all on Green Lightning. Animals, sure, but not people. Are you certain you're okay with this?"

Worry creases her brow, but she bites down on her lower lip and nods, still unable to make eye contact.

I don't like this. We haven't seen a single home or person for miles, otherwise I'd bang on the door of the nearest fae for help. The prairie has been stretching on for too long if it's led us to this fate.

I can see Des' relief before he takes a single drink. "Thank you. Thank you, Lily. I wouldn't even consider it if

I wasn't on the brink of… Thank you. I'll do my best to be gentle. You have to tell me if I'm hurting you."

I hate everything about this. I tie the horse's reins to the nearest tree, giving him a few pats on his long flank for doing the deed of toting around the passed-out General. Then I make my way over to the two, doing what I can to talk myself out of intervening.

I'm hovering. I know it, but neither Lily nor Des calls me on it. The thought of Lily being feasted on by a vampire goes against everything in me. But the very real prospect of Des dying in my arms muddies my determination tha no harm should ever come near my mate.

"I'm sorry," Des murmurs, looking up at me with guilt in his eyes. "I didn't mean for this to happen. I already consumed my emergency supply of dried blood yesterday."

"No," I rule, though as I give my edict, I'm not sure I'm right. In fact, I'm certain I'm wrong to keep Des from sustenance that comes to him voluntarily. "Ye can't drink from her. An open wound while we're on the road? She could get an infection. If she's weakened from too much blood loss, then what?"

Her body will make more, ye hovering baby. I know I'm being irrational, but I can't sit back and do nothing. What if Des does it wrong? He just said he's never fed from a person before. What if he really hurts her? Breaks a vein she needs tha won't easily repair? Then what?

It's Lily's hand on my arm tha stills the churning in my gut. It's not exactly words, but she's communicating nonetheless. The chaos in my chest settles by degrees. I take in the determination in her eyes tha trumps her fear, but doesn't erase it completely. Her eyes tell me to go, to spare me the sight of what I know I don't want to see.

If she wants me to leave when she might be in danger, she'll have to order me away, which we both know she's too depressed to do right now.

So I stay. My hands help her lay on the grass, making sure to choose the thickest, softest patch. Though, to be fair, all grass in Faveda is soft enough to be a pillow to cradle weary heads. Nature-affinity beings are spoiled by their surroundings. It's no wonder they're not bothered by the problems of the rest of the world.

I take Lily's lavender hair in my fist and twist it away from her neck, so Des doesn't pick the wrong vein by mistake. Stinking moonlight. There's barely enough light to see anything.

Now I'm sweating, pursing my lips through panic tha churns like vomit in my gut. I'm trying to keep my cool, but it's a bad act. When Des lays next to her, barely able to prop himself up with his one good arm, I'm unable to curb the anxiety tha spills from my lips. "Careful, Des. Just enough to keep ye going, not more than tha. You're going to hurt her. Don't bite too hard. But if it's not hard enough, ye might tear more things. Precision. Quick and painless, aye?"

Jays, I sound annoying, even to myself, but I don't care. I care tha Lily is safe.

Lily looks dead to the world as she lays on her back, the fire in her blue eyes dulling to a blasé "I guess this is my life now," kind of vacant stare up at the stars. I can't stand to see her like this. A fresh wave of fury comes over me, and I fight down the urge to beat her da into an early grave. He deserves it for all he's done to her, trying to kill her twice now.

Patience. Lily hasn't lived in a land with laws in a long time. If she's going to rule, she'll need to, well, abide by the rules. Murder isn't the best choice when imprisonment is an option.

Though it is tempting.

Des opens his mouth over the juncture between her neck and shoulder, but pauses and frowns up at me when a whine of terror leaks from between my lips. "You're making me even more nervous, Salem. Seriously, I love her just as much as you do, mate. I don't *want* to do this. I *have* to, and you hovering like this is only making things worse."

He's right, but I can't hold myself back. "I know, but I can't leave. Do your thing, just make it quick. This is as calm as I get when a vampire's about to suck the life out of the lass I love."

Des' jaw tightens. "I love her, too, you know. I know this mate bond is new, and it's messing with everything inside of you right now, but you have to see me, too. I *have* to live through this if we're going to unite the territories." He looks down at her innocent face, and then presses his nose into her cheek, inhaling the sweet scent of her creamy skin. Maybe some people might argue the three claw marks across the side of her face are flaws. Those people are stupid, and I'll cheerfully to beat them to a bloody pulp for saying anything bad about my mate. Des kisses her cheek with a sadness I feel deep in my bones. "She's my wife, Salem. I'll be careful."

Being mated to my best friends' wife isn't easy, but we've been managing thus far. I'm making things worse than they have to be, but I can't stop myself.

"I'm not even sure this will work." Des touches his lips to the shell of her ear and whispers, "Thank you for letting me try."

Then, before I can give him five more reasons why he can't do this to her, Des opens his mouth and bites down on tha tender spot in the curve on the side of her neck. A soft gasp flies from her lips in time with her eyes widening, taking in the full expanse of the starry sky. Her eyes flick from side to side as breath comes in ragged pants and rough bursts. She's been mute and despondent for days, but now her hips move against the night air like she's trying to get some satisfaction through the layer of denim. Her fingers tangle in his hair and tug. I'm ready to intervene if it looks like she's trying to push him away, but she doesn't. She holds his face tighter to her neck, giving with more enthusiasm as her eyes roll back with something tha can't be anything other than pleasure.

The waves of her hips and her blood are coaxing sexual moans from my best friend, who swallows with his eyes shut tight, like he's in the best kind of pain. He undulates against her side, goading her on. It's carnal and strange, and the first sign of life she's exhibited in days.

My heart is breaking, like the whole of me might be in

full cardiac distress. I don't like any man near her, and though I understand Des belongs to her, so do I. I guess I haven't reconciled her marriages as much as I'd thought. It's an ocean of confusion, wanting Des to live and also wanting to tear his head off. I'm shaking. My whole body is vibrating with two very different urges.

I want to pull him off of her, but just before I'm ready to yank him back, Des rolls to the side, a trail of blood dotting his cheek as he touches his belly, finally sated.

In the next breath, I've got Lily gathered up in my arms. I run her away from the General, away from Des, and away from the visual I never want to endure again. She's limp in my arms when I finally stop running. I slump with my back against a tree, terrified and horrified. I don't like to part with the napkins she gave me on my visits to her pub. I know it's pathetic to keep mementos of something tha was so very nothing, but every word she said to me back when she was my waitress is precious, so I wrote it down. Every interaction for five years has a napkin dedicated to it, with my penmanship spelling out each word she spoke to me. Most of them are in my safe back home, but I keep a stash on me in my breast pocket at all times, ensuring she's close to my heart.

As I take one out and use it to blot the two puncture wounds on her neck, my tight scrawl stares up at me as it quickly stains with her blood. *"Here's your usual, Prince Salem. Can I get you anything else tonight?"* The memory of Lily with her lavender curls bound up atop her head and her waitress apron draped across her hips smacks me across the face. I don't want to forget tha moment, tha span of time before I pushed her to marry my best friends. I don't regret the path we're on, but I also loathe its necessity. I didn't think I had a shot with her, and now this perfect creature is my mate.

My mate tha's bleeding in my arms.

"I'm sorry," I plead. "I shouldn't have let Des do tha. The blood's clotting okay, but it was all wrong. I'm sorry!"

Lily still doesn't speak; she merely lifts her hand to touch my cheek, looking into my eyes with the briefest brush of clarity breaking through her haze. I want her to speak to me, even if it's to cuss me out. But she's not ready, so she gives me tha small touch before she slips back into her oblivion.

I bury my sins and my nose in her cheek, promising I'll give her a better life than this. I rock us both, forward and back. I'm buried in untold amounts of pain because of those two small pinpricks on her neck.

Damn ye, Alex. Ye did this to her.